FINDING OUT

BALLARAT CHARTER LILA ROSE

Finding Out Copyright © 2014 by Lila Rose

Hawks MC: Ballarat Charter: Book 2.5

Cover Photo: Rachel Morgan

Editing: Hot Tree Editing

Interior Design: Rogena Mitchell-Jones

Finding Out is a work of fiction. All names, characters, events and places found in this book are either from the author's imagination or used fictitiously. Any similarity to persons live or dead, actual events, locations, or organizations is entirely coincidental and not intended by the author.

Second Edition 2019

ISBN: 978-0648481683

To Jessica and Chris, the best cover couple, thank you for your help and putting up with me through it all!

*O*nline dating. Some were for it and some against. Me? I was somewhere in the middle. You see, I joined the *'Find Your Soul-Mate'* dating site six months ago. Although, I'd never been on since filling out the form, until today. The reason being, I had no other choice now. I was desperate. My cousin's wedding was creeping up slowly, and I had just over a week to find a date to take.

The truth, I had lied, and now it was coming back to bite me on my huge arse. I'd told my bitchy cousin Leanne I was bringing my long-time hot, successful boyfriend Max. The only problem was he didn't exist. This left me scrolling through the list of potential victims who could accompany me on this date and pretend we'd been an item for two years.

The door to my office—out the back of the café I owned— opened and in strolled Helen, my best friend since we wore diapers. She looked great in her pantsuit. The sight of her had me thinking that I wished I'd have said I was a lesbian. At least then, I could have taken Helen, and we would have had a fun night. Instead, it was just going to be awkward. Especially since my parents were flying in from Sydney to go to the wedding, and they couldn't wait to meet my *serious* boyfriend.

Yes, I had lied to them as well. In my defense, my mum kept hounding me about marriage and babies. They thought having a twenty-eight-year-old single daughter was wrong. That was only because my younger brother and sister were both happily married off.

Arguably, the happy part was still debatable.

Dragging the chair in front of my desk around next to me, Helen sat down. She slapped my hand away from my mouth because she hated my habit of chewing my nails, seemingly oblivious to my worrying over my whole life falling apart.

She pulled her long blonde hair up and tied it into a pony-tail on the top of her head. She was beautiful, with her sexy hair, bedroom deep-blue eyes, and Jessica Rabbit figure. Turning gay was still an option; I could just say that Helen won my heart away from my serious, fake boyfriend.

She cleared her throat before she spoke. "No, I will not take one for the team and become gay for you, even for one night."

"Poop," I sighed.

"Come on, Ivy. You'll find someone perfect who will make your she-bitch-from-hell who-is-actually-a-guy and sucks-cock-like-the-dirty-tramp she is cousin choke on her own tongue."

Did you feel the hate? Not that I could blame her, Leanne did steal Helen's fella, who she was now marrying. I even hated my cousin for it, and I refused to go to her wedding until my mum rang and threatened that since I was the only cousin living in Ballarat, I was to attend no matter the situation or else she was going to post on Facebook that she wished me well on my sex change. Yeah, my mum could be a bitch.

"I can only hope," I muttered and slumped back in my seat as Helen pulled my laptop closer to her.

"Oh, look at this one. He's got a nice profile picture. It says, 'Hi, my name is Nick, and I love pussy.' Okay, maybe not that one," she giggled. I rolled my eyes. Some men were true idiots. "Look at this. You haven't even opened your message box. Mr Right could be sitting in there waiting for you. Let's see."

I didn't bother looking. Helen lived an orderly life and I hoped she'd help...all right, take control of this and just point me in the right direction. Though, I was actually surprised people had messaged me. My profile picture was not that good. I'd uploaded the one where Helen had just said something funny, and I was laughing hard while we were out at a park with my German Sheppard Trixie. My brown eyes were squinty, and my long, wavy, mousy-coloured hair was blowing in the breeze, which meant it was everywhere, including over my face and a bit in my mouth. Still, six months ago Helen had insisted on that photo. She'd said it would let a man know that I was fun and full of life. I honestly thought she was full of shit. Now I thought she was only half-full of shit. I had messages in my box. I wish I had something else in my box...it had been too long since it was last filled.

"Right, you have two potentials out of ten. The other eight are just scary and will not be worth mentioning."

I sat up and adjusted my jeans and tee. Just because I owned a café, it didn't mean I had to dress like the boss. I would hate to wear something like Helen wore every day at her journalism job. My café was all about being comfy. If I was happy and comfy, then I hoped it meant my workers would be, as well as my patrons.

"Hit me with the good ones then," I said. She moved the laptop so we could both see the screen. When my eyes landed on the profile picture in front of me, I uttered, "Holy shit, I wish I was a virgin again so I could lose it to this guy."

"I know," Helen sighed. She shook her head and continued with, "Here's what he's written about himself. My name is Fox Kilpatrick. I'm thirty-eight years old, and I work in construction. I'm looking for someone who is fun and lively. I like to go to the movies, cook and clean."

I snorted. "No way would a guy say he likes to clean. Either his sister filled this out, or there is something seriously wrong with the man."

Helen shrugged. "Maybe to both, but even if there was something wrong with him, just imagine turning up to *her* wedding with that on your arm."

This was true. Fox was definitely a fox. His eyes shone blue, and he had shaved head that showed his dark blond colour. To top it off, like frosting on a cake, he had a small smirk upon his full lips that said he had a sense of mischief inside of him.

Me wanty.

"Before you fall for this one, take a look at option two. His name is Jim. He's a doctor, works long hours but is looking for someone special enough to understand that what he does is important. In his free time, he likes to ride, eat out and also relax in with a good movie, while cuddling."

"Oh," I sighed. "He sounds nice and a doctor is very important, so I already understand he'd be a busy man."

Helen turned to me and asked, "What did you tell your family your mystery guy did for a living?"

Biting my bottom lip, I mumbled, "A cop."

"Ivvvvy," Helen whined. "You shouldn't have told them anything. Next time, and yes I know there will be a next time, be vague. Say he does a bit of this and that."

"I was under pressure. You know I don't work well when under pressure. It was the first thing that popped into my head when mum asked. Plus I was watching *CSI* at the time she called."

"Well, thank God, you didn't say pathologists."

Raising my eyebrows, I queried, "Huh?"

Rolling her eyes at me, she smiled and answered, "A person who works on dead people."

"Oooooh, well, I wouldn't have said that. That's just gross."

She shook her head and laughed. "You're an idiot. Now, I suggest having a date with both of them. That way after meeting them, you can pick out which one would be better at lying to your family."

"Good thinking ninety-nine. But for now, I better get back out front before Justine and Manny kill each other." My employees were school dropouts, and no one had given them a chance to prove themselves in a job. Therefore, I did. If it weren't for the sexual hate/love tension between the two, things would be perfect.

"All right, but you will message them back tonight? You need time to work on them both before doom-day."

"Totally, I will not fly solo to this gig and have all my happiness in life sucked from my body."

"Glad we have an understanding." Helen smiled. We did our usual secret handshake and butt slap, and she left me to go save my shop.

After I shut down the computer, I walked out of my office and into the front of my café just in time to hear Justine hiss at Manny, "I'm going to kill you slowly and painfully if you stuff up another coffee." I didn't mind the death threats. I was used to them, and so were my regular customers. They even got a chuckle out of it, and I was sure sometimes they only came to get the free entertainment for the day.

I stood beside them as they glared at each other before I placed a hand on a shoulder each. "Justine, you can't kill Manny."

She rolled her eyes and snapped, "Why?"

"I'd hate to train anyone new, and I'm sure you would too."

She puffed out her cheeks and sighed, "Fine."

"Miss M, you also forget that Justine would be lost and lonely without me because she loves me so much, which is why she's always a raging bitch." Manny smirked at Justine.

Before she could find something to stab him with, I quickly said, "Manny, go and get the cupcakes from the back kitchen that I made earlier and load the sandwiches into the fridge before the lunchtime rush. Justine, please go and serve the customers and I'll make coffees for a while. Sound good?"

"Sure, Miss M." Manny grinned. He patted me on the

shoulder and slapped Justine on the butt quickly before he ran out the back to safety.

"One day I will murder him," Justine announced.

The waiting customer turned to her friend and whispered, "And one day she will screw him."

"You!" Justine yelled at the blonde businesswoman. "That will never happen, and if you say something like that again, you'll be on my shit list. Now, what in the hell do you want?"

They laughed because they knew, like Manny and I knew that Justine's bark was much worse than her bite.

I loved my workers, regulars and even those customers who popped in just for a quick coffee on the run. Most of all, I loved my café. I'd bought it five years ago when I was fresh out of university after receiving a business degree. Back then, it had been a corner milk bar, but it just wasn't busy since a supermarket moved in down the road. I think it also had to do with the fact that the owners were now in jail for selling drugs as a side business from the store.

Now instead of the gloomy look it had, it was all bright and full of life. I had pretty much gutted the inside, thanks to all the money I had saved selling my homemade jewellery online. People were sad when I stopped doing it, but to make my café successful, I had to put all my time and money into it. I was so glad I did. I wouldn't say 'Ivy's Brunch' was booming, but I am now living comfortably and have two great employees when they weren't trying to flirt in their own weird way.

The day turned out like it had every other day: we worked our butts off, me especially when Justine caught Manny staring down her top. Let's just say that Manny may come into work tomorrow with a limp. After cleaning and closing the shop, I walked the block home and relaxed in the bath with Trixie—who was happy because I fed her as soon as I got home—sitting beside me. She waited like the loyal, sweet dog she was.

Later that night, as I sat in bed, I fired up my laptop and sent a quick message to Fox and Jim. They weren't online, and before they could get back on, I quickly shut it down and then left myself pondering if they had yet replied. I eventually fell asleep in the early hours.

Bleary-eyed, the first thing I did when I woke was check the computer. Okay, that was a lie. The first thing I did was pee, and then I made myself a coffee. While I waited for that, I turned on the laptop at my kitchen table.

My heart beat like a maniac. I had two messages. I opened Jim's first. For some reason, I was more nervous about Fox's response. Jim had typed back—to my asking him for coffee at my work, not that I said it was my business place, but I just felt safer meeting strangers there. He said that he'd love to meet for a coffee and that he was available this Saturday. I replied with *'Great, I'll meet you there at ten am.'* That would give me time to chat before I helped out with the lunch.

Now my hands shook as I clicked on the next message. Fox replied to my message with a short answer of, *'Yes, see you at 2pm Saturday.'* I giggled with glee. Why did I have that reaction with one man and not the other? All I knew was I couldn't wait until two pm Saturday. What I had to do now was keep myself occupied for two days, figure out what to wear and pray that Justine and Manny would behave themselves enough while I had my blind dates.

I was on my way to work when I texted Helen telling her that I was all organised for Saturday with Foxy and Jimbo. She asked if she could pretend to be a customer in the background while she checked them out. I told her that was fine because it would also help my nerves. She was also a good judge of character and could help me determine which would be more suitable to put up with my effed up family.

CHAPTER TWO

Saturday came too soon, and I found myself sitting at a table with sweaty palms, dressed in a dark blue sundress and sandals. God, I hoped to Christ Jim didn't want to shake my hand. If he did, we might be stuck together from the amount of sweat my hands were producing. I looked over at Helen. She sat three tables away dressed in jeans and a tee. She caught my eye and mouthed, 'Relax.' I nodded, picked up a napkin and wiped my hands for the fourth time. Jim was late. It was now 10:15. I hated people who couldn't be on time, but then I had to take into count that he was a doctor and could have been called away on an emergency.

So as I waited, I looked around my café to the long front counter that was off to the right of the entrance. It held the coffee machine and the cabinet of cupcakes, cookies, sandwiches, and croissants. I loved to bake. Justine and Manny were serving customers; there was a line-up of four people. Still, my eyes took no notice of them and moved on to the seating area. I had managed to fit in four booths along the opposite wall to the counter and had tables and chairs scattered here, there and everywhere in the flooring space that was left. In the long shop window, to the left of the entrance, I had a bench with chairs, where I sat papers and magazines off at both ends.

I looked back at the clock that sat just behind the register. It was now ten-thirty. It was time to give up; Jim wasn't coming. Just as I stood, Helen was beside me and said, "I just logged onto the site. He's sent you a message. It says that he can't make it, but he'd love to reschedule for Monday at the same time."

Nodding, I said, "I kind of guessed that. Can you send a quick message back saying okay?" She gave me a chin lift and typed something into her phone while I added, "Doesn't matter. I just hope Fox turns up."

She looked up at me and smiled. "I can tell by your voice that you already have a mild crush on him."

"Oh no, Helen, it's lust. Just from his picture my woman bits are crying to be near him."

She laughed. "I completely understand that. Listen, I've got to go and run some errands, but I'll be back here before your next date."

"Thanks, babe," I said. We did our handshake, and after she left, I spent my time doing what I loved: working.

"Good luck with this one," Justine started as she placed a latte on my table. "The offer still stands. If you wink twice, I'll come over here and pretend to be your jealous girlfriend to get you out of the date."

Maybe I should just take Justine to the wedding. Then the night could end up with her in jail when she discovers what douches my family members were.

"Thank you. I'll let you know." I smiled up at her.

"Great." She grinned, turned and went back to work behind the counter—after punching Manny in the arm.

It was five minutes to two and Helen had sent me a text saying she was running late; she'd be there as soon as she could. So when the bell over the door jingled, I looked up from my latte expecting it to be Helen. Instead, in walked a man who made my cooter want to jump from my body to run over and rub up against his leg. It was in heat. He also caused my breasts to tingle, which has never happened before. I shook my fogged head and realised that the man who walked in, dressed in dark jeans, a black tee—that showed off his wonderful tattooed arms—and motorcycle boots, was the man of my porno dreams and Mr Fox Kilpatrick himself. All of a sudden, my mouth went dry. I assumed it was because all the liquid from my body had travelled south to pool in my panties from the mere sight of the man before me. I watched his eyes scan the shop and then land on me.

I gulped, and with wide eyes, I watched him stalk his way over. He stopped just beside me, and in a deep voice, with a hint of a growl, he said, "Ivy, right?"

And I said, "Huh?"

His serious face stayed serious, still I caught the little lift in the corner of his mouth. I only saw it because I happened to be staring at his mouth-watering lips. He pulled out the chair opposite me and turned it backwards to straddle it. His hands rested on the top of the chair, and he stared a piercing stare straight to my heart.

"So?" he said.

That was when I vomited, not actual spew, but in a sense, only with words. That's right... I vomited words right in his face.

"Hi, yes... I'm... ah, Ivy and I guess you're Fox, right? I mean, I hope I don't have that wrong, you are Fox, right?" He sent me a chin lift, and I continued puking works, "Thank you for agreeing to meet me, you...um...I mean. I didn't think you would. You are extremely good looking and, well, you saw my photo. I don't really know why I joined the site. I mean I do. It's been a long time since I've had sex. Oh, my God, I did not just say that. I did. God, I did." My hands went to my glowing cheeks.

"Let me explain. I didn't join the site to just have sex with random guys." I grabbed my latte for something to do or else they would be running through his thick hair. "I joined...dammit; I may as well just come out and say it. I need a date...not for sex, though that would be good." I reached my hand up and shook it in front of me. "Not that you have to have sex with me. What I'm trying to say is I joined ages ago but was too scared to get on, and now I have no choice." I took a breath and placed my hands in my lap. "I'm really nervous if you couldn't tell...did I mention you're good looking and that it's making me nervous and the way you're staring at me without saying anything...I ramble in situations like this, and I can't seem to help myself." Another breath. "I was meaning to tell you...that I need a date, for my bitchy cousin's wedding that's coming up. *That's* why I got the courage to get back on that site."

I snapped my lips shut. Oh God, was I getting an eye twitch? Hell. Yes, I was. There it went again and again. Shit.

Next thing I heard was something being slammed down, and then Justine was stomping our way. Oh, sweet Jesus and Joseph. She thought I was winking at her. I waved my hands up in front of me, and with wide eyes, I said, "Justine, no it's fine. At least I think it is." The poor guy hadn't even said a word. I just knew he was going to run for the hills.

Justine stopped beside us and asked, "So I don't need to pretend to be your gay partner?"

Fuck me.

Sighing, my head flopped forward, so my chin rested against my chest. "No, Justine, but thank you," I uttered.

"Well good," she said and leaned closer to me. "He is sex on legs, Ivy. I'd stoop him." With that, she turned and walked off.

Holy shit.

"I hav'ta get goin'," Fox said and stood up, moving to the side of the table.

I didn't look up at him, only nodded and whispered, "I understand." He was way out of my league.

"Tonight, I'll pick you up here at five. We're going out to dinner."

My head snapped up. "Are you crazy?" I asked. After everything he just witnessed, I was sure I'd lost any chance of anything.

Crossing his muscled arms over his chest, he grunted. "No. I like what I see in you. We go out and talk. 'Bout your cousin's weddin', 'bout why I joined the site and...'bout us havin' sex."

I swore as soon as the word sex left his sweet mouth I was jabbed in the snatch by an invisible dick because I nearly came on the spot.

He smirked. "Five?"

I nodded and then whispered, "Five."

His parting word was, "Good." Then he left.

Two seconds later, Helen walked in, she took one look at me and uttered, "Shit, you're a goner." She came over and sat in the seat Fox vacated. "He wasn't here long. Was he an arse? It doesn't look like he was. You're all... moony."

"No—" I began, only to stop when Manny walked up and placed a piece of paper on the table.

"Miss M, this was left for you on another table."

I smiled up at him. "Thank you." I unfolded the paper that held my name on the front. It read, *The way you acted with that man was disgusting.* Scoffing I scrunched the paper up and placed it in my coffee cup.

"What was that?" Helen asked.

"Nothing really, I think it was from one of my family members popping in to annoy me." I rolled my eyes.

She snorted. "Annoying." Helen sang, and then smiled. "Come on, I need you to tell me the sweet stuff. Tell me *everything*." She leaned forward, her head in her hands with her elbows on the table.

"Well...." I started only to stop when there was a loud commotion at the front counter.

"I don't give a fuck about the policy and that you can't divulge information like that. I know the fuckin' owner is Ivy

Morrison. Just point me in the right goddamn way to see her," A beautiful blonde yelled at Justine over the counter.

"Fuck you," Justine hissed with a glare in her green eyes.

The blonde laughed and said, 'I like you. You got fire. But, sweetheart, you won't win against me."

"Jeesh, Satan with a pussy, the girl is doing her job. Leave her be," a tall, obviously gay man said from beside the blonde.

"Dee, calm down and listen to Julian," a dark-haired woman sighed. "Miss, thank you for your help—"

"She wasn't any bloody help," the girl named Dee snapped.

Before she could scare any customers away or before Justine jumped the counter and attacked the foul-mouthed woman, I stood from the table and called, "Excuse me." The three of them turned to face me. "Is there anything *I* can help you with? I am the owner, Ivy Morrison."

"Well fuck me sideways," Dee smiled.

"Oh, bless my gay heart, aren't you pretty." Julian grinned, and as the dark-haired lady made her way over to me, the other two followed.

She held out her hand and beamed. "Hi, I'm Zara. I was wondering if we could have a chat?"

I looked from one smiling face to another and then nodded, gesturing to the table where Helen was still sitting. Julian pulled up a chair from another table, and Dee sat on one side, while Zara, who was just as gorgeous as Dee, sat on the other side of me.

"So, is there a problem you have with my café?"

"No," Zara answered and then introduced herself to Helen.

"Hi, I'm Helen, Ivy's best friend."

"I'm Deanna, but most call me Dee."

"Or Hell Mouth, slutguts, hooker, sponge cake...oh, I could go on and on." Julian smiled and then shook Helen's offered hand. "I'm Julian. I just came along for the ride with these two interfering crazies."

"Whatever, gay man." Dee snorted. "You love this shit just as much as us."

I cleared my throat. "And what is *this*?" I questioned.

"You just had a date with Killer right?" Zara asked.

"Killer?"

"Sorry, I mean Fox."

"How is it that you know all their first names and I don't?" Dee asked Zara.

"Because I have a heart and I care."

Dee shrugged and rolled her eyes. "I have a heart...now."

Zara patted her hand and said, "You do, honey, you do, and I'm so happy for you."

Oh, my God. What in the hell is going on? Who were these nice freaks?

"What in the hell is going on?" I asked.

"Sorry," Zara said, "you see, we just wanted to make sure you were okay after the date with Killer or as you know him Fox."

My heart started tap dancing. "Shouldn't I be?" I squeaked.

"Yes, no, um...Yes," Zara stuttered, "the thing is, Fox lost a bet with his biker brothers—"

"He's a biker?" I gasped.

"Well, yes, but a nice one...sort of. Anyway, what I was saying was that after he lost the bet, he was dared to join this dating site and go on at least one date and you were it. I just wanted to make sure he treated you right. Sometimes he can be a bit…broody and abrupt or not talk at all."

Julian and Deanna nodded along with Zara.

"He, um, he was fine?" I said, making it sound like a question.

Helen scoffed. "She was more than fine. At first glance when I arrived, he'd already left, but when I spotted Ivy here, she was off in la-la land. I think she fell already and hard."

"Hoo-boy." Julian clapped.

"Awesome." Dee smiled.

"What happened?" Zara asked.

"That's what I want to know," Helen said.

"Well…" I fidgeted in my seat. "You see, he really didn't get a chance to say much." I bit my lip and then spewed once again. "I get nervous around good-looking people, not that you all aren't good looking because you are, and if I was I'd be checking you out more. Anyway, I have a tendency to ramble when I'm nervous, which is what I did with Fox and I ended up telling him my plan—"

"Oh, God," Helen moaned in sympathy. She knew all about my ramblings.

"I mentioned to him that I just really needed a date for my bitchy cousin's wedding and something about not having sex in a long time. Though I did say I didn't go to the site to just have sex, it was all because I need to find a date for the wedding." I took a breath and looked at their wide eyes. "Then, he said he had to go. But that he was going to be here at five to take me to dinner where we will talk about why he was on the site, my cousin's wedding and… um, intercourse."

"Holy sex on wheels, I wish I was there to hear that. I mean Killer is smoking hot," Julian said.

Deanna and Zara shared a look, a look that caused them to smile. That look and smile had me on edge.

"What?" I asked. "What's that look about?" I pointed from one woman to another.

"Nothin'," Dee smirked.

"Should I be worried about this?" I squawked. "I mean, he's a biker. Aren't bikers bad guys? Oh, my God, did he get his name from being a killer? Do I need to run and hide?"

Zara placed her hand over mine. "Honey, no to all of the above. You have nothing to fear from this man. Sure he *is* broody and snappy, but it's obvious you have caught his attention and honestly," —she looked to Dee and then back— "we're glad. He's a nice guy, Ivy, and yes he may be a biker, but the Hawks MC Club members are good men. I should know, I married their president."

My eye widened. "You did?"

"Yes and he's wonderful, sweet, kind, but bossy and all alpha male. Deanna has just gotten engaged to another biker too."

"You are?"

"Hell yes, they're hot." She grinned.

I turned to Julian and asked, "What about you?"

"Oh no, lovey, I'm not married, engaged or doing any bikers. My partner is Zara's brother, and he runs in his own kind of hotness. Though, I do have to say...not many bikers would put up with my," he waved his hands over himself "whole greatness, but these men do, and it just proves how special these women's snatches are. These bikers love and devote their time and lives to their women. If I weren't with Mattie, I'd try and snag me one, because then I'd know I'd be safe and loved for the rest of my gay life. Not that I won't be with Mattie. He is possessive and manly hot," he sighed, smiling.

Wow. These men sounded wonderful.

"Are you going to go on this date with Fox?" Helen asked me.

They all waited with baited breath for my answer. I already knew I would, even after I found out he was a broody biker. However, these three awesome people had sold me on Fox.

Smiling, I said, "Yes."

Helen smiled back at me.

Julian squealed. Deanna yelled, "Fuck yeah." And Zara quietly said, "Yay," with a big smile upon her face.

CHAPTER THREE

My afternoon was very bizarre. I left Justine and Manny in charge while I went home to find something to wear.

I wasn't alone though.

No, Helen and my three new friends all followed me the block to my house. While Julian, with Trixie, my dog, at his side, riffled through my wardrobe looking for something for me to wear, I sat at the kitchen table with Zara standing in front of me as she applied my makeup. Helen was sitting opposite us gabbing with Deanna.

How was it possible that we had only met these three people hours ago, yet it already felt like we'd known them for years?

"Okay, I'm nearly done. It's not too much, so you don't look like a..."

"Hooker," Deanna supplied for Zara.

"Yes." Zara nodded. She picked up my makeup mirror

from the table and held it out in front of me. "What do you think?" she asked.

"Oh, my," I sighed. She had done a wonderful job. It was delicate and subtle. Just perfect. "I love it, thank you."

She beamed down at me. "My pleasure. Julian," she called down the hall. Trixie came running. When we had walked through my front door, and Julian started cooing over Trixie, she hadn't left his side.

"What, cabbage breath?" Julian answered.

"We'd better get going soon, get your skinny butt out here." She helped me tidy the makeup as she explained, "I can't leave the twins with Talon for too long, and it's already been an hour."

"You have twins?" I gushed.

"Sure do..." she paused to grin, "and Maya who's seven and Cody who's thirteen, one big, happy family."

"That sounds wonderful. What about you, Deanna, do you have any children?" I asked.

She smiled a warm smile, her eyes softening. "Yes, my man has a two-year-old. Her name is Swan."

We heard Julian's shoes clip-clopping down the wooden hallway floor when he said, "And don't forget you're trying for your own little demon. God knows I'd never get out of bed if I was trying to get knocked up with Griz's kid." He laughed as he walked around the corner carrying a red and white sundress.

I gulped. "Really?"

"Shit, yes," Deanna said.

"Killer will love that on you," Zara added.

"And maybe you'll get more than a sentence out of him."
Julian grinned.

"You'll look smoking hot in that, Ivy." Helen smiled.

I ARRIVED BACK at work in the red-and-white sunflower dress.
My hair was loose and wavy, my makeup minimal and pretty.
I teamed my outfit with black ballet slippers. In case the night
grew cold, I also brought along a black jacket. As soon as I
was through the door, Manny wolf-whistled, and Justine
clapped and said, "You look hot, Ivy."

Blushing, I replied, "Um, thanks. Is everything nearly
ready for lock-up?"

"Sure is, Miss M. But I doubt you'll be checking everything
twice before *you* leave."

"Why do you say that?"

Manny gestured with his chin just as the bell jingled as the
door opened. I turned to find Fox standing in the doorway.
His body had stilled, except for his eyes. No, they ran along
my body and finally landed on my face. "You ready?" he asked.

My body sagged. I was a little deflated from his reaction. I
guess that maybe he wasn't happy with what he saw.

Justine must have seen this, and I was thankful that no one
else, besides Manny, was in the store when she hissed, "Don't
be a jerk. You just eye fucked her, now tell her how much you
like what you see."

"Justine—" I started.

"Justine," Manny warned. He grabbed her hand and pulled

until she stood behind him. I was wondering why he'd done that until I saw Fox's face. It looked like he was about to verbally rip shreds through Justine. His lip was raised, his brows drawn together and a growl rumbled from within his chest.

"Fuck," he snapped. "This is why I don't do this datin' shit." He took a step forward, wrapped an arm around my waist and pulled me close. His mouth met mine. It was hard and possessive, and when his tongue ran over my bottom lip, I gasped. He took the chance to force his tongue into my mouth, which I liked, a lot. Coming out of my shocked state, I wrapped my arms around his neck and gripped him tightly to me.

He growled from deep within. I moaned and then a throat cleared behind us. Fox pulled away and I whimpered. He ignored our audience, and with our faces close, he uttered, "You look edible. In fact, you taste like cupcakes, and I want fuckin' more."

I whimpered again.

"Wow, oh wow, oh wow." I heard Justine say behind me.

"Now, are you ready?" Fox asked.

"Um... yes?" I said and made it sound like a question because honestly, I wasn't sure I was ready for Fox Kilpatrick.

He smirked for a second and then it disappeared. He looked behind me and said, "Later." He took my hand and turned back to the door.

I looked over my shoulder to a worried Manny and a smiling Justine and said, "You'll both be okay?"

"Oh, we'll be fine, Ivy. Have fun," Justine sang.

I managed a nod before we were out the door and in front of his black Jeep.

He opened the passenger door for me and nodded to it. "In," he stated.

Biting my bottom lip to hide my smile, I thought of what Zara, Deanna, and Julian had said. They were right. Fox was a man of minimal words. Climbing in, he shut the door, and I got to admire the view of Fox in black jeans and a white tee as he walked around the front of his car and then climbed in.

"Um," I started, "where are we going?"

There's a seafood joint a few blocks away. Hell, do you even like seafood?" he asked. Worry marred his face with drawn brows.

"Yes, I do. It sounds nice."

He looked at me and then back to the road. "Good."

It didn't take us long to get there. Soon enough, we were seated opposite each other with a menu in front of us. I knew *I* was studying the menu, but I could feel Fox's gaze on me.

Looking up, I asked, "Do you know what you want?"

"Yes," he growled.

My eyes widened. The heated stare told me that I was what he wanted.

"Ah... okay, I mean, um. What do you want to eat?" I blushed when he smirked. "On the menu... in front of you," I clarified. "Because the seafood basket for two looks good. Would you share at all? You don't have to, you're a big guy, and…so you probably like to eat a lot. I don't know if that will be enough for you... ah, is it?"

"Sounds good." He gestured with his head to the waiter. Once he came over, Fox ordered for us. He also ordered us both a beer to drink, which I liked. I wasn't a wine or champagne drinker. After the waiter disappeared, Fox said, "Let's talk about why I was on the site."

Playing with the napkin in my lap, I informed him, "Oh, I already know."

"How?" he growled.

I bit my inner cheek and told him, "I met Zara, Deanna, and Julian this afternoon. They told me all about the bet you made before Zara gave birth. I would have done the same and guessed both boys," I mumbled.

He closed his eyes and uttered, "Fuck."

Clearing my throat, he opened his eyes to glare. I continue when I saw his jaw clenched with anger, "No, it's okay. They, ah, they're really nice people. I like them, and they obviously care about you and... um, all the men in your group."

He rolled his eyes. "They like to stick their noses where they shouldn't."

"Well, at least I spoke to them, because, um, now I'm not so nervous about you being in your group and... I, you seem nice, and you're very good looking. I know I've said that and I... you must get a lot of attention from women... I don't know where I was going with that statement," I admitted.

He studied me with a small smile upon his face. "I like it when you get all flustered."

My eyes widened. "You do?"

"Yes," he said with a nod. "So I guess I won't be tearing through the three musketeers for interfering if it means you're here because of whatever they said."

I licked my lips. "Yes, I mean, I'm glad I met them, and yes, they helped me be here, but...."

"But?" he asked.

"I knew I was going to come as soon as you asked me, no matter what."

His eyes flared with surprise. I had shocked him.

"I'm glad then, cupcake," he whispered.

Had he just called me cupcake?

"Cupcake?" I asked

"Yeah, cupcake because you make 'em, because you smell like 'em, and because you taste like 'em. You're fuckin' lucky we're out in public, or I'd be demanding more of a taste from you."

That was intense and so damned hot in a scary, stomach-fluttering, happy way. I didn't know if that made sense, but right then I didn't care.

"Okay," I whispered.

"Okay to what?"

"Um...." I looked around the restaurant and then back to Fox's heated gaze. "Okay to everything."

"Good." He smiled, and this time, for the first time, it did reach his eyes. "Now, let's talk about your bitch cousin and her wedding. Then we can move onto the subject of sex."

My cheeks blushed. Immediately, I wanted to hide under the table. But then hiding under the table made me think of the fact that Fox's crotch would be down there, and then that made me think of his penis and me undoing his zipper, taking his cock into my mouth.

"Oh, God, is it hot in here?" I asked before I took a big gulp of water from my glass.

"No," he chuckled.

Nodding, I put the glass back on the table and looked to my side as the waiter placed the seafood platter for two in front of us. As we both started to munch, I began to talk... not a good sign.

"So, um… as you know I have my cousin's wedding to go to and its next weekend. But you see, I don't reeeeally want to go. Though, if I don't turn up, my mum will publicly be congratulating me about my sex change on Facebook." He coughed on his mouthful. "Yes, she can be evil. She's like the rest of them; they all think their shit don't stink." I sighed and took a bite of a prawn while thinking. "I love them, of course I do; they're my family. But they annoy the hell out of me and can be... um, cruel in ways." I looked up from my plate with wide eyes. "Oh God, have I just scared you away from the whole thing? Of course, it's totally up to you if you want to go or not. Or, even, I mean...you might not want anything to do with me after this first date... shit, I have to stop talking. I talk too much. It's your fault." I waved my hand that held a shrimp stick at him. "You're too... everything. Sorry," I mumbled and turned my gaze away.

"Finished?" Fox asked.

I glanced back, then away again and asked, "Do you mean eating or talking?" I looked back at the platter in front of us. "I could do with more food." I picked up a scallop in some sauce and sucked it back.

"I meant talking, even though it turns me the fuck on listening to your voice."

"Oh," I whispered.

"Ivy, finally, I'm fuckin' pleased that my brothers made me go through with a bet or else I wouldn't have met you, and from what I see, I like you, a lot. So much so, I'm willin' to put up with your family at this goddamn wedding."

Grinning widely, I asked, "Really?"

He watched my mouth, and in turn, his own lips formed another smile for me before he said, "Hell yes."

With fisted hands in front of me, I did a little jig and uttered, "Yay."

He chuckled. "Christ, you're cute. Now let's finish this meal."

While we ate we chatted, okay, I mainly did all the talking, but at least when I asked questions, Fox answered them. So I ended up finding out that he was in construction. He was part owner of his company with another member from the Hawks MC club named Stoke. He also, when he could, worked in the mechanic business at the bikers' compound. He lived on his own on some land in the suburb of Nerrina; he had no other family members besides his biker brothers. He joined Hawks after meeting Talon five years ago and learned that Talon ran things differently than other biker clubs. Fox wanted to be a part of the cleaner, safer living. He said he wouldn't have it any other way because what he had before he met Talon was shit.

That made me sad.

I think he saw this because after the waiter had cleared away our plates, he stated, "I want in you tonight. What are your thoughts on that?"

So of course, all sadness from that moment fled, and instead, I clenched my legs together so I wouldn't come.

He... Fox Kilpatrick, a.k.a Killer, wanted in me tonight.

He meant sex, right?

That he wanted to stick his hotdog in my bun? Right?

"Cupcake, I can see that I've shocked you." Fox smirked.

"Um...." I leaned over the table. He leaned in as well and then I whispered, "I just want to clarify what you mean. Is it... sex? You want to have sex with me tonight?"

"Yes," he growled as he reached a hand out to tuck my hair behind my ear.

As Fox kept my stare with his wild, heated one, I uttered, "Yes."

He grinned. "Good. Let's get the hell outta here before I spread your legs over this table and fuck you hard."

Leaning back, I nodded. "Ah, that's a good idea...I think." He chuckled and stood from the table. "Wait," I shouted, causing people to look at us. I took hold of Fox's wrist and pulled him around to me, where I was still sitting. Tugging him down so our noses near touched, I told him, "I... um, I don't *usually* sleep with a man on the first date. I just wanted you to know that. But, you, um, you seem to have some effect on my body... and mind," I admitted, which made me blush like a virgin on her wedding night.

"Shit, woman, I never thought I could get harder from watching you for the past two hours, but I am. *I know* you're not like that, but I'm goddamn happy that you'll be tonight, just for me." With that, he shook off my hold, took my hand and led me from the restaurant, after paying of course.

CHAPTER FOUR

ox told me his place was too far away and he couldn't wait that long to be inside me. That was why I was unlocking my front door with Fox standing at my back. Trixie came barrelling down the hallway from, no doubt, my bedroom. Usually, she'd growl or bark if I had someone new with me as she had with Deanna, Zara, and Julian. Only with Fox, she took one sniff of him, wagged her tail and whimpered up at him for a pat.

Yeah, girl, I would do the same.

"She likes you," I said as I led the way down my hall and into my kitchen. I looked behind me for Fox, only he wasn't there. I went back to the hall and glanced down it. I found him just inside the door, crouching down, patting and comforting Trixie.

My heart melted.

He looked up and said in his deep, strip-worthy, voice,

"Good because I like her owner." Then he stood and stalked toward me. "You want me, Ivy?" he growled his question.

I backed up into the kitchen where my back hit the bench.

"Ivy, I asked you a question. Answer me," he ordered as he kept coming.

"Yes," I panted. Because I sure did want him in any way I could have him.

At my words, he stopped a few steps away from me.

"Show me your bedroom, Ivy," he hissed through clenched teeth.

Studying him, with his hands clenched into tight fists, I asked, "Why did you stop, Fox?"

He closed his eyes for a moment. When he opened them, they were wild once again, this time filled with lust. "Because, cupcake, if I come at you right now, in your kitchen, I won't be able to control myself. I will be between your sweet legs fuckin' you rough, crazy and fast. I at least want you comfortable while I do it." He smirked. "Go to your room, Ivy, and I will follow, but look out when I do."

Licking my lips, I nodded. As I made my way down the hall towards the bedroom, my heart beat rapidly, and my chest rose and fell quickly. Though, on the way, I had a wicked thought. I gripped the bottom of my dress and pulled it up and over my head, dropping it to the floor, leaving me in my matching red lacy bra and panties.

I heard a hiss, growl and thump behind me. I glanced over my shoulder to see that Fox had hit the wall with an open palm. "Fuck, you just had to, didn't you!" It wasn't a question, so I said nothing. He took two long strides toward me. In the next second, I was over his shoulder and he was rushing into my room. He threw me to my bed. I bounced up and down and stared at him with wide eyes as his own eyes raked my body.

"You're so goddamn beautiful. I've never had a piece like you," he growled. He whipped his tee up over his head and threw it to the floor. His tattooed chest, stomach, and arms were the sexiest thing I had ever seen.

Rubbing my legs together, I said, "And I've never had anyone as hot as you, Fox Kilpatrick."

"Christ," he swore as he undid the button on his jeans, sliding down his zipper. "Tell me you're wet and ready for me, cupcake. Tell me?" he asked as he removed his jeans and boxers. He stood, and I watched his big, hard cock spring up.

Oh, hang on, eyes off the candy. It was hard, so very hard— pun intended—but he was waiting for an answer, so I gave him one, "I'm more than ready for you, handsome."

He nodded, kneeling on the end of the bed, only to rethink it and stood back up. Instead, he grabbed both my ankles. I let out a squeak as he pulled me down the bed toward him. He let go of my legs, and his hands went to my underwear at the crotch, where he ripped them apart and plunged two fingers inside of me. My back arched and I moaned, "God, yes."

"Damn, woman, fuckin' beautiful and wet, so tight too." He leaned over me, his hand landed on the bed beside my head as he used his other hand to fuck me. "Yeah, gorgeous, take my fingers." And I did. He ran his thumb over my clit causing me to cry out.

But then his fingers disappeared, and I watched with hooded eyes as he sucked them dry. Then I felt him lining his cock up at my entrance.

"After this, after I come inside you. No one else is allowed. You get me, Ivy?" he asked as he rubbed his cock up and down my slick lips.

"Um?" I said, because I truly wasn't focused, all I wanted was his cock inside of me.

"Ivy," he growled. I looked up at him; he seemed strained, holding back control until he got what he wanted out of me. "You take no other but me inside of you. Yes?"

"Yes," I agreed.

"Good, you on the pill?" he asked.

"Yes, babe, now fuck me already," I snapped, only to groan as he thrust forward so all of him was embedded inside of me.

"Fuck," he swore. "You okay?"

"Oh, yeah," I sighed.

"Good," he hissed against my cheek and then he moved back out to thrust back in. "Beautiful pussy, fuckin' glorious," he growled as his pace picked up and he fucked me hard and fast, just like he said he would. His lips met mine. I wrapped my arms around his neck and melded my body, as tightly as I could against his, kissing him back.

"Dammit," he hissed against my lips, and then he pulled all the way out and away from me.

"Fox?" I whined.

"You nearly had me coming already. I'm not used to that, and I don't want to blow my load just yet," he explained and then knelt on the floor between my legs. His lips, teeth, and tongue were at my center, running up and down, driving me insane.

"F-fox," my breath hitched as my orgasm built inside of me.

"That's it, gorgeous. Come for me," he ordered as he inserted two fingers inside of me and I came around them.

"Hell," I cried as I kept coming. "Yes, yes." Fox removed his fingers only to have his cock deep in me once more. As he pumped into me over and over, I mewed as I ran my hands over his smooth, built body.

"Shit, cupcake, shit. I'm gonna come. Fuck," he swore as I felt his hot seed fill me. Still, he kept pumping and then grunted. Once he stopped moving, with his hands on the bed on either side of my head, he looked down at me and growled, "No fuckin' one but me." I nodded. "Good," he stated and then pulled out of me only to place two fingers inside of me once again.

"W-what are you doing?" I asked.

"You only came once. I want another one out of you before we sleep. I'd do just about anything to you, but I won't eat my own cum, so you get my fingers again until your pussy is clamping around them," he said as he continued to drive his fingers in and out of me.

"Um...o-okay," I gasped. He leaned over me and his lips latched onto my nipple where he bit down as he ran this thumb over and over my clit.

The orgasm ripped through me. I grabbed his arm with both hands and yelled through it.

As he slipped his fingers from me, I caught him smiling down at me. I was spent. All I wanted to do was curl up and sleep.

"Cupcake, let's clean up to sleep."

"Mm-kay," I mumbled, but didn't move, then I heard his chuckle.

"Ivy, come wash up, and then we can sleep," he said, and I just knew there was a smile in his voice. I was sure he was smug because he had worn me out.

"In a sec," I answered and then snail crawled up to the end of the bed where my pillow was.

"Fuck, cute and sweet." I heard Fox laugh. Then mumbled to himself, "Never had that before."

He must have left for a while because I had drifted off until the bed was dipping and Fox said, "Lift up, cupcake, and I'll get the blanket over you." I lifted. He shifted, and then I was brought back into his arms. He curled his front around my back, and before I drifted off again, I heard, "I fuckin' love the fact you don't give a shit you're sleeping with my seed in you. Fuckin' beautiful."

MY ALARM WOKE me at seven am. I'd forgotten to turn it off last night and couldn't help but be annoyed that I was awake so early on my only day off. Until, that was, I remembered the night before. Smiling, I reached out to the spot next to me, only to find it vacant and cold. I sat up quickly, turning. Fox was gone. He must have disappeared early hours for there to be no warmth next to me.

It felt like he had taken the warmth from my body.

How stupid was I? To think that a hot, sexy tattooed man would stick around. He obviously got what he was after last night.

Slumping back on my bed, I screamed into the pillow next to me. Only it smelt like him, so I threw it across the room.

Tears prickled my eyes. No! There was no way I would be crying over my own stupidity. I threw the covers from my naked body and went for a shower with a sad Trixie at my side; she was just upset as I was that Fox had left. As I showered Fox from my body, I thought about what I was going to do regarding the wedding, *and* regarding the longing I felt for a certain Foxy man.

How could he have weaved his way into my system so quickly? I didn't have an answer for the last, but the first I knew; I was going to attend my cousin's wedding on my own. Which somehow, I didn't know how, reminded me of cancelling my date with Jim, the doctor. I was in no mood to deal with another member of the male species.

After the shower and dressing in jean shorts and an old tee —it was house cleaning day after all—I went into the kitchen and fed Trixie some dry food. She barked at me happily. At least she was easily over her mood with the thought of food. *Yeah, that's an idea. I need a good breakfast of chocolate.*

Instead, I booted up my laptop and then turned to start the coffee maker. That was when I found a piece of paper.

 Mornin' Cupcake
    Had to run, shit to do. Be back to pick you up at eleven. You're coming to a lunch thing.
    Fox

MY HANDS SHOOK. My heart beat rapidly, and I smiled so wide

my jaw hurt. Fox still wanted to see me. He still wanted... me. Okay, so my mind had pegged him as a bad-boy biker type. I'd never had one before, so of course I was shocked that he wanted more than just one night from me.

Gripping the paper to my chest, I did a jig in the kitchen like some giddy little schoolgirl. Only to stop and look at the clock above the sink. It was ten am. I had taken too long in the shower. I raced from the kitchen with Trixie at my heels, only to run back to bring up the dating site on my laptop and send a quick apology message to Jim. Trixie and I then raced back to my room to get dressed.

It was ten-to-eleven by the time I was dressed. I had changed so many times, I was sure I had whiplash. In between wardrobe changes, I remembered I'd forgotten to check my letterbox on Friday. As I walked back into the house, I found another weird letter. That one stated, again, that I was disgusting and I'd be soon paying for my behaviour. I seriously had an effed-up family. Someone—probably a certain cousin who didn't want me at her wedding so my mum would be pissed at me—was playing stupid tricks on me and I was becoming unbelievably annoyed by it. With a sigh, I threw it in the bin and grabbed something quick to eat. After I put Trixie out in the backyard for the day, I was walking toward my room for my purse when the front doorbell rang. Squealing under my breath, I couldn't have Fox hearing I was too eager I ran-walked to the front door, dressed in jeans and a white-and-blue checked cowgirl blouse.

As soon as I had the door opened, I was encased in strong tattooed arms. "Fuck, what in the hell have you done to me?" Fox growled into my hair above my ear.

"Huh?" I questioned.

He placed his forehead against mine, his hooded eyes bore into mine. "It was damn hard to leave this mornin'. All I could think about was getting' back to you. I don't do this feelin' shit. Well, I hadn't for a fuckin' long time until you." He closed his eyes. "Or this talkin' shit," he chuckled.

There went my heart again. It swooned big time for this man in front of me. This scary biker man holding me tenderly.

"I'm glad then because you have turned me upside down and inside out with feelings." I wrapped my arms around his neck and gently, slowly pulled his face closer to mine and whispered, "I like the way you make me feel, Fox Kilpatrick, a lot." Then I kissed him on my front porch for anyone to see.

He moved a step away and snapped, "Jesus, woman. Go get your shit so we can go or I'll be draggin' you inside to fuck you."

Turning my head on the side, I asked, "And that would be a problem how?"

He smirked, shook his head and said, "Nope, I told my brothers I'd be bringin' someone. They think I'm lying." He ran a finger from my temple down and across my bottom lip. "I need to prove the fuckers wrong. Let's go, cupcake."

I gulped, bit my lip and then uttered, "Y-your brothers, as in, you're biker brothers from your group."

He snorted and then chuckled, bringing me back into his arms. "Yeah, precious, my biker brothers, but it's called a club, not a group. You don't hav'ta worry about anythin' though. Nothin' will happen to you. I won't let it," My body warmed, not from just his touch, but from his protectiveness. "Besides," he continued, "Hell Mouth, Wildcat and the gay dude will be there."

The gay dude I understood. I pulled back to ask, "Hell Mouth? Wildcat?"

"Shit, that's what the brothers' call 'em. I'm talking about Deanna, she's Hell Mouth, and Zara, the boss's misses, is Wildcat."

Giggling, I said, "I can understand Hell Mouth, but Zara as Wildcat?"

"There's a story behind it, but Wildcat can explain it to you. We hav'ta get movin'."

"I'll grab my purse. Meet you at the car," I said quickly and took off to do just that. Excitement blossomed in my chest; I was getting to see Fox in his group—sorry, club situation.

As I climbed into his truck, I asked, "So do I get a nickname? I mean, will everyone call me cupcake there too?"

"Christ, no. Well, they better not. That's my name for you. I'm sure the brothers will think of somethin' else."

I beamed at him and uttered, "Cool."

He chuckled. "Fuck me, you are too cute."

CHAPTER FIVE

I had the time of my life. To start with, I'd been scared shitless when I walked into what they called a compound. It was where all biker business and meetings were attended to. The dimly lit hallway kind of freaked me out, but then we came to a large room that held a bar, couches, tables, chairs, and games. It was filled with people standing around shooting the breeze.

What also freaked me out was when we entered; Fox was in front, dragging me behind him with his hand in mine. I came to a stop beside him. If it weren't for the music playing, I would have heard cricket's chirping. The laughter and talking stopped; they all turned to take in Fox and me.

I was just about to take a step back and flee when Fox's arm came around my shoulders, He leaned his head in and whispered against my temple, "It ain't you they're starin' at. Okay, they are, but it's 'cause I don't bring women here.

Never have, never thought I would," he pulled away and looked into my eyes, "until you."

Smiling up at him, I reached my hand out, forgetting that we had a large audience and cupped his face. I said, "You keep being nice to me, you won't get rid of me."

He winked and said, "Good."

It was then someone boomed, "Well, fuck me." A guy around Fox's age came up to us. Damn it to hell. He was good looking. He held out his hand, and as I shook it, he said, "Good to fuckin' meet *you,* the killer charmer. I'm Stoke." He beamed, then let go of my hand when Fox glared at him, causing him to chuckle.

Before I could respond to the biker, three other men walked up, and shit a brick, all of them were good-looking, tattooed, biker men. "Hey, Ivy, Zara's told me all 'bout you. I'm Talon, her man. This is Griz, Deanna's man, and Blue," spunky Talon said. Again, I didn't get to reply because Talon turned to Fox and said, "Never thought I'd see the fuckin' day." He gave a chin lift and added, "It's good, brother."

Stoke cleared his throat and asked me, "What in the hell are you doin' with this ugly fucker? Baby, I could treat you better."

I knew he was teasing, but that didn't stop me, especially because they were all good-looking, which made me nervous. I said the first thing that popped into my head and then, once again, I continued spewing words, "Because he gave me multiple orgasms last night," I gasped. My hand flew to my mouth. Talon, who was sipping his beer, choked on it. Griz guffawed, Blue burst out laughing, Stoke beamed a mega-watt smile at me and Fox's arm, around my shoulders, squeezed me.

"Holy shit. I'm so sorry. That was rude and private. I shouldn't have said it, but you see, I get nervous around good-looking people, and you're all...." I waved my hand at them, "good-looking, though...." I paused and leaned in, bringing Fox with me because his arm was still around my shoulders. Noticing they didn't lean in toward me, I went on and whispered, "I'm sorry to say this, but Fox is way better." Standing up straight, I added, "Still, I get nervous and I can't help it. I've always been like that. To make it up to you for saying that you're not as good looking as Fox, you can all come to my café. I'll give you some cupcakes." I nodded and smiled.

"Fuck me, I missed out again," Blue grumbled and walked off.

Glancing at the other three men, who looked like they all wanted to laugh, I turned to look up at an amused Fox and asked, "Did I say something wrong? I mean besides the orgasm part, but something to upset him?"

"No, cupcake," he smiled.

"He's just jealous Killer got a woman before him," Stoke answered.

"Oh, well, I have a friend—"

Stoke stepped forward and growled, "Do not tell him that. Let's keep it between you and me for now. I'd love to fuckin' meet her," he smiled. I couldn't help but laugh.

"Hey, woman, good to see you here," Deanna said as she came up beside Griz and placed her arm around his waist. His arm automatically went around her shoulders, where he brought her in closer.

"Hi, Hell Mouth," I smiled.

She glared at me and then Killer, but turned back to me and ordered, "Ivy, I ain't Hell Mouth to you—"

"No, but she'll answer to slutguts, wench, hooker, sin eater... haven't we been through this? Anyway, she'll answer to just about anything else really." Julian smiled at me as he walked up to our group with a very sexy man beside him. "This is Mattie, my partner, and Zara's brother."

"Hi." I smiled and held out my hand to shake. He shook it and said, "It's nice to meet you."

Julian clapped with glee and announced, "We need a nickname for you." He then went on pondering it.

"Bitchface?" Deanna offered. I glared at her, but it was Fox who hissed, "You better fuckin' not."

Deanna smiled. "Relax, killer, I was just jesting."

"Chatter," Talon said.

"Ooooh, good one, Hawk-eye," Julian said.

"Definitely suits her," Griz laughed.

A blush finally rose to my cheeks from my earlier comments.

"Come on, Chatter. Let's go see what Zara's doing with the tribe of kids. You can meet her and Mattie's parents too." Julian grinned a cheeky I-know-something-you-don't grin. I looked to Fox who grimaced. Were Zara and Mattie's parent that bad?

"Fox?" I asked.

"Brace yourself, cupcake, brace. You think the three you met yesterday were in any way crazy... wait till you meet Wildcat's mum."

"She isn't that bad," Mattie offered.

Julian turned to his man, took both of his hands and said gently, "My sweet, sexy man, you are a part of her loins, so maybe you don't see it so much. But your dear mother is cray-cray, in a sweet, want to choke her way."

Mattie shuddered. "Please never talk of her loins again."

"I second that." Talon glared.

"But," Julian added, "alas, we love her. We truly do because she made two beautiful children. Isn't that right, Cap'," Julian asked Talon.

I giggled at him. Julian had been right. These bikers were scary, but once you were in their fold, you could see the love they had for their partners... or else there was no way in hell Julian would get away with anything he said or did.

I smiled up at Fox, who was grinning back down at me. *Does that mean I'm a part of this fold because of this man? Yes, it does. I'm not ashamed to admit I really like that.* Fox just touched his mouth to mine when Julian said, "Oh no, once you two start, I'll have to pry you both apart with a crowbar." He tugged me away from Fox's arms. I laughed when I saw the deathly glare Fox was sending Julian, who ignored it, saying to me, "I know it's all new and sweet, my little rose petal, but he has to know he's got to share you with us. It's what we do, and besides, I'm sure, by the way he watches you take everything in, you'll be getting more action between the sheets tonight."

I sure hope so.

With Deanna and Mattie following, Julian led me by my hand to the backyard. That was where I met the loud, funny, quirky, hot-man crazed Nancy, and the sweet, mild-mannered, caring Richard. I also got to meet Cody, Maya,

45

Drake and Ruby, all of them cute in their own way. Cody being the oldest took his role seriously. He watched the twins like an eagle, while he also played cards with Maya. Then I met Swan, Deanna and Griz's gorgeous little girl, who had a white head of hair. She came up with a young girl named Josie. I found out later Josie's ordeal. It was no wonder she was quiet. I was happy to hear that Zara's parents had adopted her.

The men came outside to start cooking and drinking... well, more than they were inside. Often I felt eyes on me, and every time I searched, I saw Fox watching me with a small smile upon his sexy face. If I was butter, I would have melted into a puddle.

We ate at the picnic benches outside in the warm sun. I had the best day getting to know everyone, even the other bikers seemed less and less scary to me by the end of the day. In the end, I was becoming more comfortable with them all and only had a few slip-ups of talking too much around good looking people. What was the best though was the fact that they thought nothing of it. They all accepted me as I came and I think that had a lot to do with the man I was with. I could sense that they all wanted Fox to be happy, and for some reason, they thought I was the one who was capable of doing it. I found out later, just before Fox and I left, why.

Stoke came up to me while I waited for Fox to finish talking to Talon off to the side. He stood beside me, his face serious and said, "I never thought I'd see my brother smiling again." He turned to look at me. "Keep doin' what your doin'. Be sweet, just like you are. We can all see it. We all wish we had it, but I'm fuckin' glad that it was Killer who got it. That got you. Best fuckin' bet I ever made. Making him go through it was hard, but now that he has and I see the outcome...fuck, it makes me so fuckin' happy. He's had shit in his past, which was why he was a man who didn't talk, who didn't give a shit about a lot of things. It's different now." He took my shaking hand. I hated the thought of Fox having anything shit in his life. "I just want to thank you. You've brought him back to us. If you need anything, ever, just ask. We're more than willing to help."

Tears filled my eyes. "Thank you," I whispered. "But, um...what kind of shit do you mean…for his life?" I asked.

He shook his head. "Just normal stuff. Parents were arse-holes, girlfriend died. That shit, but it's up to Killer to tell you it all."

"Okay," I uttered.

He squeezed my hands and said, "Okay." Then he smiled and let go of my hand just as Fox came up beside us.

"Everything all right, brother?" Fox asked.

"Sure, sure." Stoke grinned. "Just askin' your old woman if she wanted to dump your arse."

Fox arched an eyebrow, shook his head and looked to me.

"I said I wouldn't." I smiled and added quietly, "Ever."

Fox's eyes warmed. He stepped up to me and draped his arm around my shoulders. Walking off, arm still around me, Fox said over his shoulder to Stoke, "Later, brother."

Stoke chuckled and replied with, "Later, you lucky fucker."

Fox drove us back to my house where he got out of his car with a bag in his hand and walked me inside.

In my house, I alternated between chewing on my bottom lip and biting my fingernails as I walked into the kitchen. Fox went to the back door and let a very happy Trixie into the house.

Yes... swoon.

After giving Trixie a rubdown, he stood and looked at me. I caught the heated look as my eyes flittered from the floor to his bag, to him and back all over again. My mind was busy pondering... feelings, thoughts that worried me.

"You mind if I stay the night?"

I looked over at him, standing there with Trixie at his parted feet; he had his hands on his hips and a scowl now upon his face. Was he worried I was going to say no? There was no way I could, and to be honest, that was one thought that was scaring me a little.

"Does it worry you that this is weird?" I asked, though I didn't wait for an answer. I went on while looking at the floor. "And I mean weird because we've just met each other and I don't like the thought of not being around you. Oh, God, that sounds scary. I'm not crazy. I'm not going to be calling you all the time, questioning you. I promise, but it... all this is kind of scary. I've had boyfriends in the past," I thought I heard a growl, "but I felt nothing for them like what I feel for you, even after one day and it's scary. We hardly know each other. Shouldn't I be putting distance between us? Playing hard to get? But I've already slept with you, and hell, it was the best sex I've ever had, like ever. Dammit, I'm sorry my mouth flies off on its own. I have to learn to shut-up. I like your friends by the way. I really like them... not as much as I like you of course." I giggled. "That's just silly. They're so nice, and you all care for one another... it's good to see—"

"Ivy," Fox growled low in his throat.

I stood straight and turned to him. I looked at his throat, afraid I had just bumbled my way out of this... whatever this was with my stupid words.

"Look at me," he ordered. I did. His eyes were intense, only I couldn't work out exactly what the intensity meant. "First, I fuckin' love your ramblings. If you didn't do it, I wouldn't know how you're feeling about this shit between us, and second, you seem to tell the truth every damn time. Never stop and never make excuses for it. Third, yes it scares me how I feel about you because I hate the thought of having you out of my sight. It's serious, but it's good. And Four and fuckin' final because I want in between those sweet legs of yours... I'm glad you like my brothers and their women and families because if you didn't, it wouldn't have worked between us. This is who I am. Those are my people, and I can't change that."

"I would never ask you to," I said.

"Good," he clipped, and then he came at me.

Talking time was over.

CHAPTER SIX

*P*icking me up, I wrapped my arms and legs around him. His mouth met mine and we kissed, hard, heavy and heated while he carried me down the hall to my bedroom. With his hands on my butt, he ground his jean-clad, hard cock against my core. I arched, threw my head back and moaned.

"Fox, I need you inside me," I demanded.

He let my legs fall to the floor, his hands on my arms steadying me. After he knew I wouldn't collapse in a puddle of turned-on goo, he moved his hands to rip my cowgirl shirt from my body. In return, I pulled off his top. Our breaths were heavy with desire. I would never get enough of this beautiful specimen in front of me.

Fox reached out again and undid my jeans. He pulled them roughly from my body. Not that I minded in the slightest because I was just as rough getting his jeans off him. Though, as I was kneeling down, helping him get his feet out of his jeans I came face to face with his sausage, which looked ready to be eaten. I wound my hand around his large length. He hissed through clenched teeth. I smiled up at him as I slowly took his cock in my mouth.

"Fuck," he growled. "Damn, I love your mouth." He watched me with hooded eyes as I bobbed up and down, running my tongue all around his cock. The way he was watching me had me reaching with my other hand between my legs. A shiver ran over my body as I touched my clit. I spread my pussy lips wider and dipped two fingers into my drenched center, moaning around Fox's dick. He gripped my hair tightly; the small amount of pain turned me on even more. I'd never had a lover do that before, never felt pain while being intimate. I decided, right then, it was something I was more than willing to explore.

"That's it, precious. Fuck your pussy with your fingers," he said.

I hummed around his cock, causing him to groan. His enthusiasm sent me into a frenzy, and I drove my fingers in and out of myself faster. I brought my thumb up and rubbed my clit, ripping my mouth from Fox's dick I cried out through my orgasm.

While I was coming down, Fox picked me up, sat on the edge of the bed and brought me straight down on his erection. I gasped as he hissed, "Ride me, cupcake. Ride my cock." And I did. With his hands squeezing my hips, I gripped his shoulders and rode myself up and down his length.

"Yeah, precious, that's it. Fuck, I love your mouth, but I love your pussy even more, so tight and wet." One of his hands let go of my hips and he wound his fingers through my hair, tugging my head down so our lips touched. We devoured each other. While our mouths tasted and teased, Fox slowed my rhythm down so I was rocking slightly up and down on him.

He tore his mouth away from mine. I whimpered, but when I met his eyes, I didn't mind that he'd slowed the pace because what I saw within his eyes was so much better. He was feeling everything I was. While our bodies bonded, our hearts were mirroring the connection.

I hadn't realised I had closed my eyes until Fox ordered, "Open your eyes, cupcake. I want you to see what you do to me while I come inside your sweet pussy." Opening them, Fox's fingers reached my clit, and with a flick, I was coming again. "Open, precious." The pressure of my orgasm had me closing my eyes, but I opened them as he told me. In response, I watched his eyes soften, his brow tighten, his mouth part as he groaned through his own orgasm. His seed pumped into me and I moaned in contentment, loving every second of it.

Later in the middle of the night, I rolled in bed, still half asleep. Moments later, I felt an arm wrap around my waist and I was pulled back against a hard chest.

Warm breath tickled my neck where I felt a delicate kiss. "I like you near," Fox whispered through the room. I smiled to myself and thanked, for once in my life, my bitch-cousin, because if it weren't for her, I wouldn't be spooned by a scary, sweet, and beautiful biker man. With that smile upon my face, I fell back asleep.

As I sat in my office at my café, I thought back to my morning. Fox woke me in the early hours, even before I was due to get up, by spreading my legs and saying, "I need inside you before I have to get to work. I wanna remember your pussy milking my cock all day." He then continued to fuck me, sweet and slow, and yes, my pussy did end up milking his orgasm out of him. He then kissed me gently, but it soon turned rough before he got out of my bed naked. As I watched him walk to my bathroom, I felt like singing '*Zip-a-de-doo-dah, zip-a-dee-day, what a wonderful feeling, what a wonderful day.*'

After his shower, he came back to the bed, kissed me again and told me he'd see me later. With a smack on my butt, he walked out of the room, only to come back to inform me that he was going to feed Trixie and let her out the back.

If a man treated an animal right, you just knew he would treat you right.

Finding a man in life who made you feel different in so many nice ways was hard. What was harder was finding out that your heart already knew what it wanted even before your brain acknowledged it. Because it was right then that my mind caught up to my heart and it told me Fox Kilpatrick was the one for me.

I dozed for another hour before my alarm rang, which scared the crap out of me. Getting ready for work, I didn't even try to ignore the new spring in my step after getting me more than a little something-something all weekend long.

Later at work, I brought up the dating site for the last time as I sat at my desk with a stupid grin on my face. As I was about to delete my account, I noticed I had a message. Opening it, my heart sank to my arse.

> Ivy
> I thought you were different, but you aren't. You're just like the rest of them. I watched you fawn over that delinquent man like some slut, and then you go on a date with him and **then** fuck him. You chose the wrong man, Ivy. You are going to regret it. I'll make sure of it.
> Jim

No. No. What was I supposed to do with a message like that? Jim had seen me with Fox? Here in *my* café. He'd been watching us? He followed us. My stomach clenched at the thought of it. My heart was beating out of control. I pushed my chair back and bent over with my head between my legs, trying to steady my heart, breath, and shaky body.

I gasped... he was the one! The one who sent me those notes.

This was serious. *He* was serious.

What was he going to do?

Was he out there watching me?

What did he mean by pay for it?

Oh, my God. What do I do?

My office door opened and I heard Justine ask, "Ivy, are you okay?"

All I could do was shake my head and continue shaking it because I wasn't okay. There was no way I was okay... would I ever be again? Tears formed in my eyes and then spilled over. I was in no state of mind to stop them or my body from shaking with shock and fright.

"Ivy, what's wrong?" She sounded frantic as she tried to pull me up, but I shook her off and closed my arms around my legs as tightly as I could. I then rested my head sideways on my knees. "Manny?" Justine yelled.

"What? What is it?" he asked as he ran into the room.

"I don't know. Something is wrong with Ivy. She won't talk to me."

I closed my eyes to try to stop the tears. My stomach tightened. I closed my mouth, my lips thinning, trying to get my breath under control so I didn't lose the contents of my stomach all over the floor.

Shit, what does he mean I'm going to pay? Why me? Why this now? Fuck, he'd been to my house. He knew where I lived, where I worked.

"Miss M, what's happening? Come on, Miss M," Manny pleaded. I shook my head, and with my eyes closed, I started humming. I hated hearing their concern. It worried me and I had enough to worry about. "Get me her mobile," Manny ordered. "I'm going out front. You stay with her." Over my humming, I heard shuffling and then I felt an arm come over my back. It was small in frame so I knew it was Justine's.

"It's going to be okay. Whatever it is, it'll be fine," she assured me.

I was doubtful. No one had ever threatened me. I had no idea what to do.

Please, please…what do I do?

Sometime later, the door to my office banged open—Manny must have shut it. I jumped, but I didn't bother looking to see who it was.

"Ivy?" Fox's voice broke through it all. I opened my eyes to watch him kneel beside me so he could meet my gaze from where my head still rested on my knees. He reached out a hand and gently pushed my hair away from my face. "Cupcake, what's wrong?" His voice was gentle. I had never heard it that gentle. He was handling me with care. My scary biker man was beautiful.

"She's been like this for a while. She won't say anything. I don't know what's going on," Justine explained, her tone filled with concern.

"Ivy, please fuckin' tell me what set this off?" Fox asked.

Still, I watched him blinking. I wasn't ready to talk. I wanted to. I wanted to tell Fox everything. But I didn't. I couldn't when my own mind couldn't comprehend what was happening. I just wanted to fade…fade away so nothing could happen. Though, my heart knew it wanted to take Fox with it.

I fought with my body to keep from reaching out to Fox. I had to tell it and my heart that it wouldn't be safe for him. I needed to protect him.

But I was weak. How could I fight this… man on my own?

Fox had said he wanted to protect me….

I didn't know what to do. Everything was too hard.

Even my thoughts.

"Ivy, I need to know how to fix it, precious, please." He got nothing back from me. "Fuck," he hissed. "Fuck," he yelled.

"Brother," someone snapped, "let me try."

Fox moved out of the way, and Stoke came to his knees in front of me. He smiled. "Woman, you need to come out of this. You need to tell us what the fuck happened, because if you don't, my brother, your old man, will tear everything and everyone apart to find out what it is. He'll go fuckin' crazy doin' it too. Don't let that happen, Ivy. For him, get the fuck up and tell us what we need to know."

Oh, my God. He was right. I couldn't do that to Fox. Not after I'd only found out his brothers just got him back. I was hurting him by trying to keep him out of this. I was hurting my man by what I was doing. I blinked long and hard and then stood on shaky legs.

"That'a girl," Stoke said.

"Fox," I uttered. He turned from holding onto the door frame to me. I was in his arms in the next second. He even shoved Stoke out of the way to get to me.

"Precious, Jesus, cupcake. What the hell?" He leaned back to look at me. I placed a hand on his cheek and said, "I'm sorry for worrying you. All of you," I added as I looked at Justine.

Stoke cleared his throat and told Justine, "Give me a minute, sweetheart."

"I ain't your sweetheart," she glared, "but I'll give you a minute. Someone has to keep an eye on Manny," she said and left the office, closing the door behind her.

"Ivy?" Fox said, and my eyes went straight to him. "What happened? I left you all sweet this mornin', but then I get a phone call from the dude out front sayin' you're in a damn state. I need to know why, cupcake?"

Licking my lips, I nodded. I looked into his hard, intense

57

gaze. He was panicked and worried about me. He wanted to help, and I knew then that I really needed it. Not only that, I needed him. I couldn't let this step between Fox and me.

I raised my hand, and with one finger, I pointed to my computer. The screen had gone blank, in rest mode, but Stoke shook the mouse. He paused to read the message and whispered, *"Fuuuck.* Brother, you need to see this." Fox let go of me. I wrapped my arms around my waist trying to keep his heat on my body, but it fled.

"What the fuck?" Fox hissed. "What the fuck?" he yelled. "Shit," he said, shaking his head. He hit the deck with his fist before he turned back to me and I was pulled into his arms. "Whatever he means, it ain't gonna happen. He won't touch you. Fuck, he should never have threatened you." He looked over my shoulder to Stoke. "Make a meet with Talon. This guy is gonna go down. You get me, brother?"

"I get you. Fuck, do I get you."

"Make the call then," Fox growled. Stoke gave a stiff nod and disappeared out of the office. "No one will touch you. I will not lose you too, cupcake." His voice held a softer emotion, and it had me thinking that his thoughts were lying in the past... only, I wish I knew how he lost his first girlfriend.

It also made me think that I needed to be stronger. Not only for my sanity but also for the man with his arms around me.

"Fox..." I started.

He took a deep breath and said, "I heard Stoke telling you I had a shit past. I did. Some of it was my own fault. I don't give a shit about losing my parents. They're dead, and they're better off dead. But I had a woman once. Yeah, we were young, but I knew I loved her. We'd surrounded ourselves with the wrong people, and it caught up with us. Fuck... promise me you will not hate me for this?" He pulled me away from his chest to meet my stare. I nodded. I doubted anything could make me hate this man. "I need words, Ivy."

"Fox," I said softly, "I promise I won't hate you."

He nodded and led me over to sit in my office chair again. Kneeling in front of me, he took my hands in his. He didn't look at me. Instead, his eyes were on our hands.

"We'd partied hard, like most nights, but one night...I lost sight of her. In the end, she got raped and stabbed by two, what I fuckin' thought at the time, friends." I gasped and gripped his hands tighter. "It was my fault. I trusted the people around us, but I should have known better. My last name is *Kil*patrick, but I got my nickname Killer for how I dealt the payback. I hunted them and killed them both," he uttered.

If the tables were turned... if anything happened to Fox like that, I would have done the same. I would have found the people responsible and exacted justice. It may be crazy talk since I'd only known the man for a couple of days. Although, by the way he made my heart shimmer with love, I knew I would go beyond anything to help him. At least I wasn't crazy enough to voice it. That *could* scare my man away. I wasn't ready to risk that.

I pulled my hands from his and watched him nod his head. He thought I was rejecting him. That caused my body to react in sadness. My eyes filled with tears, my stomach tightened, and a pain in my chest appeared.

I pushed my chair back and knelt in front of him. His head came up, his eyes wide. I took his face in my hands and smiled at him. "You're a wonderful man, Fox Kilpatrick. Nothing you just told me could ever have me hating you, so get that thought out of your head. I'm scared, worried and... really, really scared. But I know, I know you will protect me with everything you have, from whatever this psycho will do, as long as you know I will do the same for you. I'll do anything to keep you safe, Fox. We've only just started this. There is no way I am willing to lose this or you."

I took a deep breath. On a roll, I kept going and felt Fox's warm eyes sink into my soul, suffusing me in heat and warmth. "Be that, I'm not ready to move in with each other or anything. We're still testing the waters. You never know, one day you could get sick of my jibber jabbering. Until then, we'll take each day as it comes... that is, after we deal with this weirdo." I stood and started pacing.

"Which I don't get. Why take a fascination in me... and how dare he call me a slut. Slut, Fox. I'm no slut. You're the first man I've slept with in... God, two years I think." Spinning toward him, I finally felt it. Anger. "This guy will ruin everything. Finally, freaking finally, I find a man, you, who will put up with me and my word spewing." I stomped my foot. "No. That guy, that loser, idiot, cocksucker will not, and I mean, will NOT ruin this. Right?" I asked with my hands on my hips, glaring down at Fox, who was smiling up at me with an amused expression.

Standing, he swooped me up into his arms and placed me on my desk. "Fuck me. How did I get so lucky? One second you're breaking, the next you're consoling me, and then you're as angry as a crazy woman. Christ, you're mental, cute and feisty."

I glared at him as he stepped closer between my legs. "You're bloody lucky I like you, Fox... like a lot, or you'd be kicked out for that crazy comment. And yes, I'm a little highly strung, and my moods can change from one to another in seconds. Are you still willing to put up with *that*?"

"Hell yes." He grinned. Even though I saw a glimmer of worry within his eyes, he still made sure I'd see the warmer emotions he had for me, right before he kissed me. I wrapped my arms and legs around him and kissed him back with just as much gusto.

A knock on the office door interrupted us.

"In," Fox barked.

The door opened, and Stoke walked in with a smile on his face. "Damn, I thought you'd have her naked by now," he complained and then chuckled when Fox picked up my stapler and threw it at him. He dodged, and with his hands in front of him, he added, "I come bearing news. Talon said no meeting required. You want protection from the brothers for your woman, it's there. Anything you need will be there if you want it. Just call and organise it."

I witnessed Fox bow his head. It was clear the loyalty of his club really meant something to him. His brothers were willing to fight at his side for me...for his woman. It also meant something to me, which was why I shouted, "Free coffee and cupcakes all round."

Later that afternoon, I dragged Fox back into my office and told him about the notes I had received. I'd completely forgotten about them after the more recent, scarier events. I

LILA ROSE

explained that I had thought it was my cousin playing pranks on me. I mentioned that we should call the police. He pulled me close and gripped me tightly. As he rested his forehead against mine, he whispered, "Do you trust me, Ivy?" I nodded. "No cops just yet. If something doesn't happen soon, we'll call them. Until then, let me and my brothers deal with it. Can you do that for me?"

Everything, but my heart, told me that this was wrong. That the police should have been called as soon as it happened. But, and that but had a huge capital b, my man, the man I wanted in my life for a very long time, he followed a path of what someone could call, different laws. The question was, now that I was with this man, was I prepared to live *my* life like his when it came to something like this?

Licking my dry lips, I answered, "Yes, but, Fox...if it doesn't work out, if you and your brothers can't find him, we will call the police, right?"

"Yeah, cupcake. Two weeks, that's all I'm asking for."

I smiled. "I can do that."

CHAPTER SEVEN

*A*s the week passed, my mood and days were similar to a vomit-inducing roller coaster. One second I'd be smiling, and that, of course, was because I was thinking of Fox and my new found friends. That was until I'd remember that I was being followed by some weirdo, and then my mood would fall into the despair. Not only because I was worried for my safety, but because of everything Fox was doing to keep me safe, not only him either, but his biker brothers and also their women. If Fox couldn't be with me, one of his brothers were, even overnight. Though, I noticed it was either a brother who was married or in a relationship.

Fox arranged for his brothers to install a security system in my house and workplace. He told me there was no way in hell this fuckhead would drive me off from the places I called home. Relief had filled me when he'd made that statement. Glad didn't even begin to cover it, so instead, I showed him by giving him the best head-job I had ever given.

Despite my week of anxiety, time didn't stand still, and Friday soon arrived, the day before the wedding. Fox had pretty much demanded that we shouldn't attend it. I told him that I had to or hell would rain down upon us. He said he could take it, but I highly doubted it, not when the hell would come from my mother. In the end, he gave in… okay, it was only after I got him all sweet when I jumped his bones and he came hard.

I learned that sex did wonders for my biker man and helped me get what I wanted. Even though I was more than happy to please him in bed, the getting my own way made it that much sweeter. Plus the multiple orgasms from both parties helped. The funny thing was, he knew exactly what my motive was, and he played along with it, smirking at me. I was also learning that I couldn't fool my man.

Helen came in Monday afternoon and yelled at me, asking why I hadn't called her to inform her of *everything.* I told her I was a little distracted and occupied, but that my man and his men were dealing with it all. She sighed and mumbled with a blush to her cheeks that she knew. Stoke had taken it upon himself to go to her work and introduce himself. He'd then filled her in on everything that happened. Yes, even the part that Fox and I have had sex. Then he asked her out. She agreed. I laughed. She glared. We cried, yelled and then we got over it together. From then on, she also called in every day and rang every night. I never felt more suffocated in my life, but I didn't mind. In fact, it all warmed my heart.

MY CAFÉ HAD GAINED MORE customers over the week. Apparently, Stoke had spread the word that one of their brothers' misses owned a café that they'd get discounted food and drinks. I did try to give it to them for free, but none of them accepted that. They paid.

My lunch times were always busy. Not only from the biker brothers but also from my new friends. Deanna, Zara, Julian, Mattie, even Zara's parents and all the children came in. It could have been a ruse to keep my mind busy; most of the time it worked. No matter what though, I loved having them come in.

The only strange thing that happened for the week—well, besides when I blundered through conversations with the good-looking bikers—was that I hadn't heard from Stupid Jim. No other email, phone call, visit or anything. Fox told me not to let my guard down. Just because he hadn't made more contact didn't mean he wasn't out there watching. I was happy that he hadn't made another move, but it also annoyed me. I wanted him out of my life for good, so I could move on with it and finally stop the daily worry.

Friday lunchtime, I was sitting at a table in my café across from a large built man. He was similar to a lumberjack wearing his blue jeans and checked shirt. His name was Butch, and he worked for a PI agency. Zara had called his company and asked for help since Fox, and the bikers were unable to find Jim. He had asked questions, and I answered them, even showing him the dating site and Jim's profile. After he took notes, smiling, laughing and making me comfortable through it all, he laid his hand over mine and his sobered, hard gaze met mine. Then he said, "We'll find the bastard." His was so sincere, the way he switched from a sweet man to a gruff looking, scary one told me that he was ready to do anything to find Jim. It also had me wondering from his severe change of moods that something could have happened in his past, something that made him aggressive to any type of abuse on a woman, a little like Fox. To reassure Butch, I smiled and nodded.

Hearing hard footfalls heading our way, we both turned. Fox, with a killer look upon his face, stalked toward us.

Ignoring Butch, he asked me, "Who's this fucker?"

I gasped and glared. "Fox, that is no way to talk. And this is Butch. He works for a PI place."

Fox turned to Butch and glared. "Talon's sister's?"

Butch glared back and said, "Yeah."

Oh, wow, bad-arse, biker boss Talon had a sister in the PI business. I felt like giggling for some reason.

Fox's eyes moved from Butch to his hand that, I then noticed, still covered mine. "So I shouldn't kill him for touchin' what's mine?" he asked as he looked from our hands to me.

I moved my hand from under Butch's and stood, curling my arms around his waist. "No, handsome, but we could talk about your possessive ways."

He smirked down at me. "Not up for discussion."

Rolling my eyes, I uttered, "Thought so." I looked down at Butch, who now seemed amused by the interaction between Fox and myself. Ignoring Butch's smirk, I added, "Sorry about him. He gets a little carried away."

Butch shook his head, stood up and said, "You bikers have all the fuckin' luck. Ivy, you rest easy. We'll find him."

"If you do, you hand him over to Hawks," Fox ordered.

Butch clenched his jaw. "Vi's already told me."

Fox smiled. "Good."

Butch gave a chin lift to both of us and left.

Fox turned me, so my front pressed against his chest. He leaned his head down so our foreheads touched and he growled, "Go to your office, Ivy. I need to fuck you. No one touches you but me. I need to fuck the thought of his touch outta my system."

My body hummed. His possessiveness was a pain sometimes, though, most of the time, it got me all hot and bothered. That was why I whispered, "Um…okay."

He took my hand and walked my dazed-self to my office. Justine gave me a knowing wink, and I watched her laugh, I smiled shyly and shrugged, though I didn't stop. Once we reached the office, Fox threw the door open. He pulled me inside, slammed the door shut and pushed me up against it as his mouth assaulted mine. His hands went to my jeans, and he popped the button. Just as I was running my hands under his tee and Fox was slowly unzipping my jeans, someone cleared their throat from behind us.

I squeaked. Fox spun fast, had a gun drawn from somewhere and pointed it at his friend's head.

Stoke laughed and said, "I guess you worked out what that dude was doing here and touching her for. Did you forget you sent me in here to wait?"

"Fuck," Fox hissed. Which told me he had forgotten.

I couldn't help but laugh. I never thought I'd see the day that Fox forgot something as his passion took over. Fox shook his head and turned back to me. "Don't you fuckin' laugh," he said with a smile, which made me giggle even more. "Goddamn, you keep up the cuteness I'll just fuck you in front of him."

My eyes widened and my lips clamped shut. But what surprised me was the tingle of lust, from the thought of someone watching us, sent me to my core. I rubbed my legs together and Fox, being so close, noticed my reaction.

"Hey, be my guest. I wouldn't mind the show," Stoke teased.

He leaned closer and whispered so Stoke wouldn't hear, "You want him to watch me take you, cupcake? Does that turn you on?"

"M-maybe...." I said and bit my bottom lip.

"Christ, it does. I don't mind having my brother watch. You're fuckin' perfect when you come. But he will not touch you. Hear me?"

"Yes," I whispered. "As long as you're sure?" I asked.

"Jesus, yes." Fox pulled my hips forward and slanted his lips across mine. He kissed me fiercely as my hands groped anywhere they could on his body.

"Ah... do you want me to leave?" Stoke asked from behind Fox. He sounded confused.

Instead of answering, Fox turned and pulled me over to the front of the desk. As I breathed heavily, he placed my hands on the desk where Stoke sat on the other side in my office chair.

Stoke licked his lips. His eyes were hooded. I gasped when my jeans were pulled roughly down my legs. "Fuck me," Stoke hissed.

"Step outta them, cupcake." I did as I was told and I was

rewarded with Fox's hands running up my legs to my butt. I felt his chin on my shoulder. I just knew he was looking at Stoke because as I watched, Stoke turned to look back at Fox. "You look. You watch, but you never fuckin' touch. She's mine. You get me?" Fox asked.

Stoke licked his lips again, and for once, he refrained from any wise cracks. His eyes were serious and held desire as he nodded slowly.

My heart rate took off. Oh, my God, this was thrilling, sexy and hot all at the same time. Never in my life had I thought it would be that wild to have someone watch as another man who I adored take me.

"You wet already, precious?" Fox asked. He didn't wait for an answer. Instead, he slid two fingers inside of me. "Fuck, you're drenched. You like to be watched, cupcake. That's damn hot." He got in closer to me, so his body leaned over mine as his fingers pushed in and out of me. "Stoke, her pussy is so ready for me. Should I take her?"

Stoke cleared his throat and uttered, "Yes."

Fox removed his fingers. I felt his hand working to undo his jeans. I moaned, my head thrusting back, as he slid his erection inside me slowly.

"Shit," Stoke whispered. I looked back down at him; his chest was rising up and down fast. Fox gripped my hips and started to move faster, pounding into me, sounds of our flesh slapping against each other echoed around the room.

"Isn't she fuckin' beautiful?" Fox asked. His arms came around my chest, and he pulled me up more. Then one hand slid down to my waist and glided over my bare stomach. My tee must have come up, Fox pushed it up further with his hand and cupped my breast, squeezing.

"Damn exquisite," Stoke answered. I opened my eyes and moved my head from Fox's shoulder to look down at Stoke. The feel of his eyes on me and Fox's cock in me was wonderful. I watched as Stoke pushed back in the chair a bit and started to rub his dick through his jeans. "Brother?" he asked.

What the question was I didn't know, but when Fox barked, "Yes," Stoke then undid his jeans and pulled his cock free of his boxers. He began to stroke himself in front of me.

"*My* Ivy likes that, Stoke. She just got wetter," Fox growled, and he was right. Fox took his hand off my breast and ran it down my body to between my legs where he rubbed my clit.

"Yes, God, yes," I moaned. I wanted to close my eyes, but I didn't. Instead, I watched as Stoke moved his hand faster and faster over his dick.

"Precious, come for me while he watches you," Fox ordered. His finger on my clit rubbed that little bit harder, driving me closer and closer to my orgasm.

"Please, God, please, harder," I begged.

Fox rubbed and slammed his cock into me harder. It was building and it was going to be big. I leaned forward and gripped the desk with my hands to brace, and then it hit me. I cried out and bit my bottom lip, humming through it as my walls milked Fox's cock. When I heard a groan come from Stoke, I looked to see him lift his tee higher as his cum shot out, landing on his stomach. I felt Fox's hot seed fill me as he swore through his orgasm.

CHAPTER EIGHT

*A*fter Stoke cleaned himself off, he stood and mumbled something about getting takeaway for their lunch, and he'd meet Fox out the front. His parting words were, "Lucky, lucky fucker." Which caused Fox to laugh.

Even though I was embarrassed by what we just did in front of him, I still yelled after him, "Bye Stoke." As I put my jeans back on.

His reply was "Later, sweetheart."

Then I turned to Fox ready to ask him some questions and tell him my worries, but he got there first. Pulling me to his chest, he shared, "Stoke and I have been mates since I joined Hawks. He was the only one I talked to. He's the only one, *the only fuckin' one*, I'd let see you half naked with my cock inside you. You like people watchin' us, I'll take you to a nightclub where we can do that, but no one touches you. If you fancy my brother watchin' us again, I can deal with that." He grinned. "I like showin' what I have off, makes me fuckin' happy that they know I get to have you when they can't. Whatever you want, whenever you want it, we'll deal, yeah?"

I licked my lips and nodded. "Okay... um, as long as no one touches you too. I wouldn't like that," I admitted. For someone to watch what we had together was a big turn on, but that was it. I wouldn't want anyone to join in or touch what was mine either. So I totally got what Fox was saying and I was all for it.

"Good, no one would ever touch me but you." His lips pressed against mine gently. "I gotta shoot off. See you tonight."

"Ah, Fox?"

"Yeah, precious?"

"The wedding's tomorrow."

"I know that, cupcake. What of it?"

"Um, do you have a suit?"

He threw his head back and laughed. I liked seeing that a whole heap. When he calmed down, he kissed me quickly and said, "Ivy, there is no way in hell I'd be caught dead in a suit, even when I'm dead. I'm a jeans man, precious, and your family will just have to deal, yeah?"

"Okay." I smiled. I could handle that. After all, he was willing to put up with my family.

"I gotta go, cupcake. Stay in the shop. Griz should be here soon."

"Yeah, handsome," I murmured against his lips, and then kissed him long, deep and hard, pulling a groan from him.

He shifted back and ran a hand down my cheek. "How is it

that we've just fucked, good and proper, but I'm already hard to go again?"

"Um?" Was all I could say because right then I really wanted to go again as well.

"Shit, Christ." He kissed me one last time and took two steps to the office door. "I'll take care of you again tonight." He smiled over his shoulder.

I clapped and uttered, "Yippee." Shaking his head, he laughed before he disappeared.

I walked around my desk and slumped down in my chair, sighing, but smiling. I really could not believe that just happened.

Oh. My. I had awesome, wonderful sex in front of Stoke and I liked it, a lot... not as much as I loved my alone time with Fox, but still, at least I discovered a new turn on for me.

After I tidied up, I walked back out to the front of my café and found Griz sitting in the corner booth so he was facing the whole store. As I made my way to the counter, I smiled and waved at him. He sent me a chin lift. I gestured with my hand up to my mouth, sipping an invisible coffee, and then with my other hand, I pretended I was munching on something. I could see his chest moving; he was chuckling at me. He gave me a wink, and I took that as a yes, so I went ahead and got him some lunch.

I was getting the hang of being a biker's woman. Now all I had to do was work out what the grunts and some of the chin lifts meant, and I'd be set—because let's face it, those men communicated in their own secret way with chin lifts.

SATURDAY MORNING, I'd woken late, and now I was running around like a mad woman or like a chicken with its head cut off. All this while Fox calmly sat at the kitchen table with his feet up on another chair sipping his coffee with an amused smile upon his lips.

"Cupcake, calm the fuck down. We have three damn hours," he said as I was going through my kitchen drawers looking for some extra bobby pins. I turned my head to glare at him and saw Trixie wander in, trot over to Fox and lay at his feet. He put his feet on the ground and bent to give her some attention.

I shook my head and went back to the dilemma. "Fox!" I screeched. "Three hours isn't going to be enough. I still have to shower, dress, and put makeup on; have breakfast because God only knows why my stupid cousin would have a wedding right at lunchtime." I turned fully to Fox with my hands on my hips. "I mean, who does that, handsome? A wedding right at lunchtime. She knows people will be starving. Why would she do that? Does she want everyone cranky?" I threw my hands up in the air. "She probably does, which means we need to feed you up before we go. I can't have you getting cranky, even though you'll get cranky having to be around my family, but I mean even crank*ier*. You'll end up killing everyone and then we'd have to go on the run... after we come back and pack and get Trixie—hmmm, maybe we should pack before we go? No, no, no, I'll just feed you up real good and calm your beast." I turned to the pantry. "Now what do you want to eat? Steak, bacon, stir-fry?"

"Cupcake?" Fox said, his voice had me looking over my shoulder to him straight away. Yes, he was laughing his arse off. "Before you have a panic attack, go and start to get ready, I'll make us something for breakfast and I'm sure as fuck ain't having steak or stir-fuckin'-fry for breakfast." He stood, came at me and pried my hands away from the cupboard doors. "Move your arse, woman, or I'll smack it."

I bit my fingernail and pondered the smacking. Would we have time? That was the question.

"Christ, woman, you keep looking at me like that, we won't make it to the fuckin' wedding. Get your arse in the shower before I change my mind about even attending your dipshit cousin's wedding."

He was serious. I could tell. Kissing him quickly, I jogged from the kitchen. Usually, Trixie would be at my heels, but she stayed with her new master. I couldn't blame her. He certainly was my master in bed.

"Don't forget to feed your beast, we need to tame him," I yelled down the hall. I knew I couldn't get an answer, so I went for my shower.

I showered and dressed in a long, shoestring strapped, black dress. I was just applying the final touches to my light make-up, just like Zara had done for me, when Fox called from the kitchen, "Cupcake, you better fuckin' come eat before we have to go or you'll be the one killing your family 'cause you're so hungry."

I smiled and made my way down the hall. Upon entering the kitchen, I heard Fox hiss, "Fuck." My eyes met his warm ones as they raked over my body. "It's gonna be the shortest wedding in damn history. We'll give 'em two hours and then I want you here on your back with my cock inside you *while* you wear that dress."

I giggled. "I guess you like the dress."

"Christ, woman, I love it. Eat so we can go and get home quicker," he ordered.

I MADE sure we sat at the back of the church for the ceremony so no one would notice us, which they didn't. It helped as I also had us in the corner. I told Fox I wanted to show him off, but I wasn't ready just yet for the questions and… evilness. He chuckled, no doubt thinking I was being over the top, but he didn't know. Once he found out, I was ready to tell him 'I told you so.'

Outside the reception room, at a ridiculously expensive hotel, I stopped Fox with a hand on his chest. He looked down at it and then to my eyes. "Um, I ah, I left out one part of information."

He closed his eyes and sighed, "What?"

"I said your name was Max and that you're a cop," I said quickly.

He opened his eyes wide, but then they turned slanty. He glared at me. *Uh oh.* "I was under pressure when I was making you up. By the way, we've been dating for two years," I added and pouted.

"Fuck me," he growled. "No, cupcake. No, we ain't fuckin' lyin', especially when I will be around for a fuckin' long time."

"Fox," I whined. "Oh, my God, please just go with it; otherwise, what am I going to tell them?"

"We'll wing it," he smiled.

"Wing it?" I yelled.

"Yeah, precious," he said, taking my hand in his while I was in shock. Opening the doors, we walked into the room.

Like the vultures they were, we were surrounded in seconds by my mother, father, Aunt Lisa—Leanne's mother, bitch-cousin herself and her new husband.

"Brace yourself, handsome, brace," I uttered out the side of my mouth, throwing his words back at him. His eyes were hard, but he grinned for me and placed his arm around my waist.

"Ivy-lee, I see you finally made it," Mum sneered. "You should have seen the ceremony. It was beautiful."

Fox looked down at me and mouthed, *'Ivy-lee.'* I shrugged. It was just my mum's way to make my name sound more elegant. I thought it sucked. Throughout my whole life, Mum always thought she was better than anyone. Even her children. To her we were a burden, she brushed us off to the cooks and cleaners, in the house I was brought up in. I think it had something to do with the fact that her parents were the same to her. My mum grew up with money and was taught at a young age not to care about anyone else but herself. She was mean and vindictive, even toward her own husband.

Dad and Mum met at a young age when she wasn't so uptight. A very long time ago, he used to be fun and caring, but she drew that out of him. Now, he was a man with no backbone. He lived his life quietly and worked long hours to get away from his wife.

Really, I was surprised that my sister, brother and I turned out half-normal when we had no love in the house as children.

"I was there, Mum. We were sitting in the back. You just didn't see me."

"Oh, I saw you." Aunt Lisa smiled, eyeing Fox. She then continued to lick her lips. I glanced at Leanna to see she was also eyeing Fox.

"Why didn't you say anything, Lisa?" Mum questioned her sister, who ignored her.

"So this is your mystery man, Max?" Dad asked.

"Um.…" I began.

"No. I'm Fox *Kil*patrick. I'm your daughter's new man. We've been dating for nearly two weeks now."

"Really and what happened to Max?" Mum asked, the look on her face told me she never believed my lie in the first place. Her next words backed that look up. "You may as well come clean. I knew no one would date you for two years. You're too annoying, even as a child." My cousin laughed. Dad sighed and walked off to the bar while my Aunt still eye-fucked my fella.

"It's true," Leanne added. "You never could keep down a boyfriend. They only wanted you for one thing. God knows why," she looked me up and down, "and once they got that, they took off. Pitiful really."

"Oh, come now. Let's not forget Lester," Aunt Lisa said. They all laughed.

I groaned. Lester was our neighbour when I was fourteen. I had a major crush on him, and he pretended to like me because my mum and Aunt paid him to.

"So let me guess, dear," Mum started. "This here.…" she gestured to Fox with her hand and a gleam in her eye. Even she liked the way Fox looked. ".…is a friend of a friend

78

helping my poor child out, so she didn't look like a fool in front of her family. She has always been the lost soul of the family. The black sheep that no one could handle being around for too long." She moved to Fox's side and took his arm, leaning into his side. "That is so sweet of you," she cooed. "Let me know if you need anything. I'm more than willing to help."

Fox raised his top lip at her and shook her off. He stepped back bringing me with him. He looked down at me and glared.

"Sorry," I uttered because I was so very sorry. Being there was all a mistake. I should never have put him up to this, made him put up with my family. No one, none of my friends liked them; hell, I didn't even like them.

"Cupcake," he growled.

"Did he just call *her* cupcake?" Leanne gasped. "More like a mountain cake. Her arse looks like she eats a whole heap of them. Why did you even make me invite her?" she whined, no doubt to her mother.

"Because we had to show that we can understand when it came to people like her."

"Fuckin' enough," Fox barked.

"Fox," I started.

"No, precious, you don't put up with that. My woman doesn't put up with that, even if they are fuckin' family."

"Keep your voice down, young man," Mum warned.

"No." He let go of me and stepped up to Mum with Aunt Lisa and Leanne beside her. "You do not talk to my woman like that. From now on, you will be sweet and charming to her. I don't give a fuck if you're her mother or not. If I see or feel her body tense once more because of words you, any of you, have spoken to her, then I will make you pay. My woman, Christ, *your* daughter, is the best thing to happen to my life. You don't even deserve to be in her presence. But she's too kind for her own good and came to this shit, over-the-fuckin'-top wedding." Fox took a step back and held my hand. "You threaten her again into something like this, you'll be hearing from me," he warned. All of them were frozen in shocked states. The room was quiet. There were several eyes on us, and then, from the bar, came clapping.

I turned wide-eyed to my father, who was smiling big and clapping. "Here, here," he said.

I tugged on Fox's hand. He looked down at me and said, "Your mum's a bitch. Your Aunt's a bitch, and so's your cousin. Fuck, precious, next time I'll take your warning. You wanna get out of here?" he asked, turning us, so we faced each other.

Grinning huge, I laughed and shook my head. "You have made my day."

"Good," he grunted.

"And I'm sure you'll make my night even better."

His eyes warmed instantly. "Fuck yeah."

"So I'll need food for energy. Let's eat their food and drink their booze, then we'll get out of here."

He chuckled and said, "Sounds like a plan."

THE PLAN HAD BEEN GOOD. We ate. We laughed, and even my father came to talk to us. He told me he was proud I'd found a man who was willing to take care of me and protect me from anyone, even our family. He then told me he was going to file for a divorce. I gasped in surprise and gripped Fox's hand hard. I never thought I would see the day my father grew some balls. I was glad to witness it. He said he couldn't take her attitude any longer and that he wished he had stood up for my siblings and me as my man did, a long time ago. He hated himself for it and asked for my forgiveness. He also told me he hoped I was willing to spend more time with him. He looked to Fox after asking that.

Fox, who was leaning back in his chair with his arm along the back of my chair, said, "It's up to Ivy."

Dad looked back at me. I smiled and said, "I would really like that."

"Thank you," he answered, emotion in his voice. He hugged me and disappeared from the reception.

The plan that we had went to shit when I told Fox I was running to the loo before we left. They were inside the reception room so I guess we both thought everything would be fine, and really, I had been lulled into a sense of safeness being around Fox and hearing nothing from Jim.

I was wrong.

Opening the door to the bathroom, someone shoved me from behind. I went flying. Thankfully, the sink was in front of me and I managed to grab it before I sprawled on the floor.

"What the—" I began.

"Shut the fuck up, you stupid slut." I turned to find the man I once saw from his profile picture online. Jim was standing there with a knife held out, pointed at me.

CHAPTER NINE

KILLER

I was waiting for Ivy by the doors so we could get the fuck outta this fucked-up reception. I wanted to get back to her place and pound into her. I was already hard just thinkin' about it. Shit, let's face it; my dick was hard as soon as she walked outta her room in that goddamn dress.

My thoughts soon changed. I had been waiting on a call all night to see if Vi, Talon's sister, had any more luck finding the cockhead antagonisin' my woman. She said she had a lead. Obviously, that didn't pan out, which pissed me off. I just wished her shit would be over. I wanted someone to find the fucker who threatened her, so I could beat the hell outta him for scaring her.

She was right though. There was no way in hell this prick would ruin what we had goin' on. It had been fuckin' years, *years* since my dead heart woke from its doze. Now that it had, because of Ivy, I was ready to protect it and her in every fuckin' way. Which meant I was willing to do anything to get this fucker out of her life so we could move the fuck on and *then* I'd tell her I was movin' in permanently.

From past experiences, there was no time worth wastin'. When you saw what you wanted, you went for it, and I had. I wanted it around me all the damn time. I wanted Ivy around me as much as I could, and that meant one of us was shiftin' places, likely me.

My phone rang from my pocket. I fished it out and flipped it open, "Yeah?"

"Where in the fuck are you? Tell me, brother, that Ivy is at your side?" Stoke growled over the noise of a movin' vehicle.

"She went to the bathroom. What in the hell, Stoke?" Drawing my hand into a fist, my brows drew down. I was annoyed by his question. He knew where we were, yet a panic settled deep with my gut.

"Find her. Get her, Killer. He's there. The fucker is there. Billy just called. He was knocked out outside the fuckin' reception place. He's there, man."

"Christ," I yelled. The people in the room paused to watch me. I didn't give a shit. I ran for the ladies' room and ripped the door open. "FUCK!" I bellowed. "He's got her. The window's open. They're outside on the move. I'm heading out." I punched my fist into the wall. Pulling away my hand, dust and shit flew everywhere from the hole I'd left behind. No sooner had I done it, I was on the move again. I had to get to her. I had to find her...I just had to.

"We're a minute away. Billy should be out there. Go, brother, go."

I threw the front doors open and bolted around the side on the gravel road in the car park and suddenly came to an abrupt halt.

"What the fuck?" I whispered.

The dick with my woman spun toward me, away from Billy, who was holding a gun to the wanker. But as he spun, the knife at Ivy's throat cut into her, causing her to cry out. I watched as blood dripped down her neck.

"Move away. Back off now or I'll kill her."

"What in the world?"

Christ. Ivy's whore of a mother walked up beside me, others gathered around. Jim moved their bodies so he could see both Billy and me.

"You need to back the fuck up and take your hands off my woman."

"H-handsome," Ivy started. I watched her swallow. "There's no use talking any sense into him. I've tried."

"Shut up you slut," Jim screamed, shaking her.

"Dammit, that hurt," Ivy complained. "And I'm not a slut. I never was and never have been. I hadn't even had sex for two years before I met Fox. Two years, Jim."

I rolled my eyes. Bloody hell my woman could talk at any inappropriate time. I pulled my gun from the back of my jeans and pointed it at him. "I won't say it again. Let her go and we won't kill you."

"Can someone please tell me what is going on?" Ivy's mum snapped.

"Shut it, woman," I hissed.

She put her hand on her hips and said, "I will not shut it. A man has a knife to my daughter's throat." She looked toward Jim. "Who are you and what are you doing? I can't believe you brought this trouble here Ivy-lee. It's disgusting."

Fuck. Just that statement had me wanting to punch the bitch out. Too damn bad I didn't hit women. I was seriously thinkin' about changing that for a second. For once, I wished Hell Mouth was around. She could have done it for me.

"Really, Mum?" Ivy glared. She tugged at Jim's arm at her throat.

"You all need to shut the fuck up, or I *will* kill her," Jim screamed.

A van came barrelling around the corner and stopped. I smiled. My brothers were here. The door to the van opened, and Griz got out, Talon came around from the other side, and from the back of the van, came Stoke, Blue, and Pick. All had their guns out and aimed at Jim.

Jim looked about ready to piss himself. I could see sweat beads on his brow. His hand now shook at Ivy's throat.

"Oooooh, someone's going to get it," Ivy sang.

"Jesus, precious. How about you don't tease the fucker while you have a knife at your throat."

She looked like she was pondering the damn thought and then she said, "Good idea."

"W-who are you all?" Jim stuttered.

"You played with the wrong woman, Jim," Talon started. "She belongs to us. She's Hawks."

Jim actually squeaked like a little girl, causing my brothers to laugh. There was no way I would laugh until my woman was outta harm's way.

"Blue?" I called.

"Yeah, brother?"

"Can you and Pick get these people out of here?" I asked. If something was gonna go down, we didn't need the witnesses.

"Everyone clear the fuck out. Now," Blue yelled.

Most moved all except Ivy's damned mother.

"I'm not going anywhere," she said.

"Fine," I barked.

Just then another car came around the corner, a sleek Mercedes. As soon as it stopped, out hopped Vi, her man, Travis, and Butch.

Vi walked up and stood to the front of the bikers. She pulled her gun out and pointed it at Jim and my woman.

"Jim Coben, you are under arrest for the murder of three women. Come in quietly or not," she shrugged. "My brother and his crew will take care of you."

"Y-you can't do that. Cops can't threaten people."

Vi smiled. "I'm not a cop. I'm just a PI."

"You are the shit." Ivy smiled. My brothers once again chuckled around me. "We so have to have coffee one day. I want to hear all about your PI days. Oh, hey, Butch." She waved. She fuckin' waved like nothin' was really going down. Like she didn't have a goddamn knife at her throat.

"Ivy," I growled.

"Yeah, yeah. Right, I'll stay quiet now while this dick has me. But can we hurry this along? I was on a happy high earlier, but it's fading."

"Holy shit," I heard Billy utter. I was thinkin' that same fuckin' thing. Could my woman never shut the hell up?

"Dammit, Ivy," I snapped.

"Don't you snap at me, Fox Kilpatrick," she barked back. "Sorry, sorry just a little tense here, right…" She made a zipping motion across her lips.

"Hang on." We all groaned when she started up again. Jim yelled for her to shut up. She told him no.

"I think I like her." Vi grinned.

"What do you mean, Vi, by Jim is under arrest for murder?"

"The cops have been looking for him for the last three months. He's done this to three other girls from that dating site."

"You met on a dating site," Ivy's mum screeched.

"T-three other women?" Ivy stuttered. "Three?" She moved her head slightly, making the blade dig in.

"Cupcake, please," I asked.

"You've hurt three other women." Her tone was low, a mix of sadness and a hint of anger.

"And they deserved everything they got. Stupid sluts."

Ivy looked back at me. She had tears in her eyes for women she never knew.

"Ivy," I warned.

"Handsome, he can't keep doing this."

"And we'll take care of it," I said. I just knew she was forming some sort of plan in her head.

"Fox, you know that isn't going to work until I'm out of the way."

"Ivy, whatever you're thinkin', fuckin' don't," Talon ordered.

Ivy closed her eyes, and when she opened them, they looked so sad it hurt me to my core. "Don't," I uttered.

She didn't listen. She pulled her head down causing the knife to slice her throat more, and then brought her head back hard, hitting Jim in the nose. He dropped her, gripping his nose. As my brothers jumped him, I went for Ivy, who had fallen to the ground.

Laying my gun on the ground, I reached for her arms and rolled her over. Blood flowed from her neck. Ripping off my tee, I held it against it.

"Get her to the car, Killer. The car," Vi yelled beside me. I picked her up and ran to the car where Travis was already waiting in the driver's side.

I climbed in the back with Ivy on my lap. She looked up at me and smiled. She went to talk, but I shushed her. "No, precious, don't. I'll tell you how fuckin' foolish you were later, and then you can tell me how sorry you are." *Fuck, fuck, fuck.* My tee was soaked with her blood. I applied more pressure, trying not to hurt her. She reached her hand up and touched my cheek. She was in pain and bleeding, yet she was still trying to comfort me.

Christ.

"I'm movin' into your place, cupcake. After this, I'm movin' in, and you will not say anything about it." I told her as her eyes started to close. "No, no, no, Ivy, precious, keep your eyes open for me. Fuck, please, keep them open for me." I blinked and blinked, but the stupid tears wouldn't go away. I turned my head to wipe them on my shoulder. "That's it, cupcake. Keep your eyes on me. Good girl."

"We're here. I'll get someone to help," Travis said and then vanished.

"When this is over, I'm gonna tan your arse," I promised at

her temple. "You have my heart to take care of, Ivy Morrison. I need you, so don't go gettin' any ideas, woman. I need you because you're my other half. You stay with me," I croaked as the passenger door opened and emergency staff pulled her from my arms. It was then I realised she was unconscious.

EPILOGUE

*F*ox didn't lie. After I got out of the hospital, with my neck bandaged up hiding eleven stitches, he moved in. The earlier days in the hospital were still a blur because I was that doped up on drugs for the pain. Still, Fox Kilpatrick, my biker man never left my side, unless it was to shower. He even had his biker brothers bring food for us because he said the hospital food was shit. I told them not to bother, but they also said that they wanted to come and visit me anyway. I thought that was sweet.

My mum had come to visit me. I woke to find Fox standing in the doorway growling at her saying she wasn't welcome. It was only hours before I fell asleep that Fox, yet again, told me my mum was a bitch. At the incident, she showed no concern for me at all. Blue mentioned to Fox that he watched her turn up her nose and stalk back into the reception to continue the night as nothing happened. Like her daughter hadn't been rushed to the hospital.

So there were a few things I wanted to say to her, which was why I said, "Handsome, let her come in."

Fox looked over his shoulder to me. Once I gave him a thumbs up, he moved aside and Mum glided into the room like the blood-sucking vampire she was.

"Ivy-lee, I'm really not happy with your choice in a man. Did you know he was in a biker club? A biker club for God's sake. I understand you tie yourself to anyone who shows a bit of interest in you, but really, you need to find someone mentally stable." She took my hand in hers, leaned in and whispered, "I'm sorry I didn't get here any sooner. I had things to do. But now I'm here, you can tell that hooligan to clear out and that you never want to see him again." She stood and nodded at me.

I removed my hand from hers and wiped it on the sheet. I glanced over at Fox and smiled. Right there, standing in his usual jeans and tight tee that showed his beautiful body, was my future. There was no way I would ever want to get rid of him.

I looked back to Mum. My voice clear and strong, I said, "No, Mum."

She gasped and then snapped, "What do you mean *no*?"

"I mean no. I'm not getting rid of the man who cares for me. He may be a biker man, but I love that about him. I love his friends, his family, his possessiveness, his crankiness and I love that he can communicate what he wants without words. All I have to do is look at him." Tears pooled in my eyes. "I love that man, Mum. He's my future and I'm sorry to say, you're my past, a past I can do without in my life."

"What?" she screeched, her face contorting.

Fox took a step forward, but I waved him off and continued, "Mum, it's been four days and you haven't seen me. You
didn't even come to the hospital after what happened. Dad
did. He came, but you didn't. You don't really care. What you
do care about is what other people think. You care that I
embarrassed you." I licked my lips, feeling tired again. I
wanted to sleep, but I needed to finish this. "Do you know
what, Mum? My man hasn't left my side. He was even pushed
to shower and change clothes because he was worried I'd
wake and he wouldn't be here. Do you know how I know
this? Because his friends told me. They've all been here. Not
only them but their women as well. They have shown me
more love and warmth in the last week than I've ever felt in
my life," I sighed. "I love you, Mum, of course I do. But I can't
be around you. I'm sorry." Even though sadness filled me, I
couldn't help but feel like a heavy weight had been lifted from
my shoulders.

"You were always a self-centered little shit, Ivy. I'll be glad
to have you out of my life."

"You fuckin' bitch," Fox barked. "Get out! Get the fuck out
now before I remove you myself." Stepping toward her, she
dodged around him and left.

Fox came to my side, sat down on the seat and took my
hand. "Your mum's a bitch, precious."

I laughed, but it hurt. My hand went to my throat. "I
know, handsome. I know."

"So… you love me?" He smiled.

"You weren't supposed to hear that. It's too soon." I
grinned. He got up and leaned over, so our noses touched.
Before he could say anything, I continued, "But of course I

love the man who told me I held his heart and that I was his other half."

"You heard that?"

"Yes," I uttered.

His eyes were soft, softer than I had ever seen. "Good," he stated. "Because I meant every word. You're crazy, but I wouldn't be without you. I fuckin' love you, too, cupcake." A sob caught in my throat. Tears broke, and my man kissed them away before his lips gently touched mine.

On the fourth day in hospital, I woke to find Fox at my side sitting in a chair. He said I could be getting a visit from the police soon. He'd held them at bay until I was more myself, and hadn't mentioned anything earlier, wanting me to recover. No sooner had he told me that, there was a knock at my door. The police had arrived. I never asked Fox what was done with Jim. But when they asked me to identify the man who attacked me, I was shocked. I mumbled a yes, and they brought forward a picture. It was of Jim, battered and bruised. I looked at Fox. He smirked and winked. The proof was right in front of me. They did hand him over to the authorities, and I was glad. I wanted him judged for what he did to the other women. Though, from the picture, it looked like Fox had time for a little payback himself. I was amazed I wasn't repulsed by my man beating another. I hated violence. This confirmed I was absolutely at peace with Fox and the way he worked through situations. I was at peace because I knew deep down that Jim deserved it for what he did. Not only to me but for taking the lives of three women.

When I got out of the hospital, Fox took me home. I walked in to find a very happy Trixie. She bounced around and barked. Once I gave her enough attention, she settled. I left Fox in the kitchen to go and have a lay down on my bed. That was when I discovered Fox had moved in. I went to dump my bag in my closet and found his clothing hanging. I bit my bottom lip to keep myself from squealing with glee. I walked out of the closet to see him leaning against the doorframe.

"Do not say one word. It's happenin'. Get over it," Fox said.

I shrugged, took off my tee, removed my jeans and then lay on the bed. "I'm tired, handsome, so you're going to have to do all the work."

"Christ," he barked. I smiled over at him. Desire raced through my body as he removed his clothes quickly. He got on the bed and hovered over me. "You good then? You don't care I moved in?"

"No, I don't mind at all. Now get to work, Mr Kilpatrick."

"I'm on it," he grinned. I arched so he could unhook my bra. He slowly bought it down my arms and flung it somewhere in the room. Intense eyes stared down at me. Then with one hand, he cupped my breast. I sighed. He smiled as he lowered his mouth to my nipple and sucked it in, swirling his tongue around it.

"Yes, handsome, that feels good."

"You'll feel even better soon," he growled.

"Promises, promises."

"Don't get cheeky on me, woman. I still owe you a tanning." I didn't get to reply. Instead, his mouth met mine, and he kissed me hard, only to gentle it by running his tongue along my lips as his hand made its way down my stomach to in-between my legs. He pulled my panties aside and ran a finger over my lower lips, separating them. Our kiss turned urgent as soon as he entered two fingers inside of me. I moved one hand from his shoulder down to grip him through his boxers. He groaned. I panted around his lips as he drove his fingers faster in and out of me.

"Fox," I mumbled against his lips. He moved back. "I want you inside of me when I come."

"Fuck, yes." He was too eager even to remove his boxers. I supposed it had been a week since we'd had sex, so I couldn't help but giggle when he ripped my panties from me and shoved his boxers down, without removing them completely. He spread my legs further, and he glided inside of me. I sighed content.

"Jesus, cupcake, I love seein' that look upon your face as you take my cock. Fuckin' beautiful," he said as he slowly pushed and withdrew from my wet pussy.

"Handsome, I need it hard and fast," I moaned as he pushed deep and hit my G-spot.

"No. I might hurt you."

I opened my eyes and glared up at my man. "If you don't fuck me hard and fast, it'll be another two weeks before you get any."

"Bullshit, you love this."

"I do, Fox. I do." He kept going slowly and gently. "Okay, handsome, let me say this then. Fuck me hard and fast, Fox Kilpatrick or I'll have Julian here for dinner every night for a week."

"Christ, woman, you play dirty."

"That's because I like it dirty," I said.

He smirked. "All right, precious. Brace." I did. I moved my

arm above my head and held onto the headboard. He lifted my hips by his hand, placing it on my butt and slammed into me. His thrusts were wild and crazy. I fucking loved it.

"God, yes, Fox, yes. Like that," I moaned.

"Play with your pussy, Ivy. Touch yourself," he ordered.

I opened my eyes and took in his hooded eyes as he watched my hand slid down my body to my clit. I rubbed it and cried out. Fox groaned.

"I'm close, so close," I panted, but there was no way I was taking my eyes off my man. I wanted to witness him come and lose himself. His eyes were on my slicked finger as it ran over my clit faster. Raising his eyes, he smiled a smile that lit up his face.

"Mine," he growled, sending me over the edge. I forced my eyes to stay open as my walls clenched around his cock. I whimpered through it. "Fuck, you're gorgeous," he whispered. He let go of my legs and leaned down over me so he could touch his lips to mine. I was about to deepen the kiss, but he pulled back. Our eyes met, and he bit out, "I'm gonna come, precious."

"Yes," I uttered.

He kept my stare as I felt his seed flow into me. Fox grunted and pumped fast four times. As he slowed, he said, "Fuckin' love you."

"You too, handsome," I smiled.

THE ONE THING that surprised me, after the hiccup with Jim, was that I didn't have nightmares. I thought I would. People told me I would, but they never showed. I still woke in the middle of the night, but for a different reason, and it had a lot to do with Fox. Not only because he was curled tightly around me every night, but when I did wake, it was from words of love sweeping through my mind, chasing away any bad thoughts or dreams…*You have my heart to take care of, Ivy Morrison. I need you, so don't go gettin' any ideas, woman. I need you because you're my other half. You stay with me.*

You see, even in my dreams, my biker man protected me.

SNEAK PEEK — BLACK OUT

HAWKS MC BALLARAT CHARTER: BOOK 3

Chapter One

CLARINDA

Three weeks of hearing his voice and I was addicted. While my sister was busy doing whatever she had to do every Saturday for the past three weeks for her realty work, she dropped me off at a café so I wouldn't get in her way and annoy her. So for those three Saturdays, I had my ears glued to the door of that café, waiting for him to walk in and order his tall cappuccino. His voice was deep, rough and warming. His scent filled the room and made me want to wear leather and drink the men's cologne Joop, so that I could have it surrounding me all the time.

Sex.

That word never really crossed my mind. Mainly because my

first and *only* time was not worth remembering. I had been eighteen when I met *the unnameable,* and he had swooned his way into my life. I thought he was the one. He showered me with gifts and sweet words. Until I gave him my virginity. As soon as he'd donned the condom, stuck it in me—and Jesus, it had hurt so much, I was ready to punch the uncaring idiot in the throat— he'd thrust three times and grunted in my ear. The next day when I rang him, he said he didn't want to hang, that I was a lousy lay.

So anyone could understand why sex, lust or making love never crossed my mind.

Until him, the stranger in the café.

It sounded strange; I knew it did. I wasn't usually a stalker type of person, but it was a small enjoyment in my troubled life, and it wasn't harming anyone in return.

So yet another Saturday, and I found myself sitting in that café drinking a coffee and nibbling on a blueberry muffin, while I waited to get my pleasure for the day of hearing his voice.

The bell over the café door rang, heavy footsteps coming in and walking toward the front counter. I knew this with relative ease because every time I walked in, I'd counted the number of steps it took me to get to the counter to make my order. I'd also counted them to my usual table, the table my sister had shown me to on the very first time I had come here. She knew my counting game, so at least she knew from then on, I could make it in and to my seat without embarrassing myself.

I was sitting off to the left of the front counter, taking in a deep breath, and his manly scent soon filled my senses once

SNEAK PEEK — BLACK OUT

again. I had to take my fill before he walked out like he always did.

What was funny was I'd never felt the need to do it with any other customer. I hadn't cared to. Still, when he walked in that first time, there was something about the way he walked, the way he talked and the way the room had quieted and people took notice of him.

It left me wanting to know him.

However, that was something I'd never have a chance of obtaining, especially when no one took notice of me these days.

My appearance was less than to be desired. My clothes were baggy and big, while my red hair was a mess, and I wore no makeup, and sunglasses sat on my nose.

His order was called. I heard him say a rumble of a 'Thank you' and then I waited for his retreating footsteps, back to the front door.

Only, for the first time, he didn't.

He wasn't walking out of the café; he was staying. I could tell when I heard his pounding footsteps coming my way. I smiled a little because I knew I'd appreciate taking in his wonderful masculine scent a little longer.

"Hey, sugar, mind if I sit here?" he asked.

My lips pulled between my teeth. Was he talking to me? Was the place that full we'd have to share a table?

I tipped my head in his direction and said quietly, in case he wasn't talking to me, and I was about to make a fool out of myself, "I don't mind."

It's days like this I wish I could see. But I couldn't. My eyesight had been perfect until five years before, four days after my nineteenth birthday. After one tragic night—the night my older sister and I lost our parents.

On that horrid night, I ended up in a coma for a month, and when I woke, I could no longer see properly. My sister explained to me, once released from the hospital that my visual impairment was caused by carbon monoxide poisoning from being in the fire. That and the loss was a result of emotional trauma from witnessing my parents burn to death. They'd been stuck behind a locked door and couldn't escape.

The pain from the loss of my parents hurt more than any side effect or injury. Five years, and I was still feeling that loss deep inside.

It was lucky my sister hadn't been there that dreadful night, or she also would be waking every night from the same nightmares still haunting me.

The chair opposite me grated across the floor as he pulled it out and set something on the table in front of him.

Sounds were my best friend these days.

"Three weeks," he stated.

"I'm sorry?" I uttered.

"Three weeks, baby. Three weeks I've been coming here every Saturday, waiting for you to come to me to make a move. But you never have, so I thought I would."

My eyes widened behind my glasses, my mouth ajar. He had shocked me to silence as my heart went haywire behind my loose tee.

"I s'pose I should be the one to introduce myself, now that I'm finally fuckin' here in front of you."

Quickly closing my gaping mouth, I brought my bottom

lip between my teeth and bit down once again. I couldn't answer; so instead, I nodded.

"Name's Blue Skies."

A small smile tugged at my lips as I held back the inappropriate giggle. What were his parents thinking at the time they named him? I cleared my throat and whispered like it was a secret, "I'm Clarinda."

"Clarinda... Clary. I like it." I could hear the smile in his voice, and for some reason, it had me blushing. "Seems it's our first date, so I guess we should tell each other about us."

My head went back a little, again, shocked at his statement. So shocked, in fact, I laughed. "Are you sure you have the right person?" I asked after I controlled my laughter.

"Yes."

Puzzled, I asked, "How?"

"Because I have had my eyes on you for three damn Saturdays, waiting to catch your eye, waiting for you to get the courage to come talk to me, but you haven't. So now, we do this my way."

"Your way?" I asked in a whisper.

"Yeah, sugar," he said softly, "my way."

Licking my suddenly dry lips, I then said, "You sure are..."

"Cocky? Great with words? Smart? Handsome?"

Smiling, I shook my head. "I wouldn't know. I can't see," I told him and removed my sunglasses, blinking in his direction.

He hissed, "Your eyes are damn beautiful like that."

My eyes widened, *yet again*. This man in front of me sure knew how to make an impression. I wasn't sure if I liked it.

All right, I did. I guess I was more confused over why the man was saying those words to me.

Three weeks. His words rippled through my mind again.

Three weeks I've been coming here every Saturday, waiting for you to come to me to make your move. How was it...*he* possible? Was I dreaming?

Light footsteps approached our table, and a woman cleared her throat. "Hey, handsome."

Blue interrupted her to say to me, "See? I told you." I giggled. "What can I do for you, sweetheart?"

I snorted. Oh, God, he was a charmer to every lady.

"I have to go, but I just wanted to give you this," the woman said.

This was embarrassing; I just knew she was passing him her number. Even a strange woman could see it was weird Blue was sitting with me.

Actually, that was reality, and it just smacked me in the face.

I stood up and said, "I'm leaving, as well. Why don't you take my seat?"

"No," Blue growled. "Sugar, sit your arse down. We're talking. And woman, you need to go. I don't want your number... ever." He sounded disgusted; I was surprised.

Quietly feeling my way back into my seat, I sat across from him. The woman huffed and puffed, and then I listened to her retreating footsteps.

I wondered if he got that a lot. If many women picked him up wherever he went. It also made me want to know what he looked like, especially if that sort of thing *did* happen a lot.

"Stupid woman," Blue grumbled.

"I'm sure you could still chase her," I giggled.

"You, shut it," he said with a smile in his voice. "Now, tell me about Clary."

I shrugged; it was the weirdest situation I had ever been in. No man had ever approached me before. "There isn't much to say."

"What do you like to do?" he asked.

"Read—I mean, listen to audiobooks." I smiled. "What do *you* like to do, Blue?"

"I'd fuckin' love to know—" His phone rang, cutting him off. "Christ," he swore and answered it with a gruff, "What? Shit. Yeah, all right, I'm comin'." I heard him shut his phone and slam it to the table. "I have to go."

"That's okay."

"No, it ain't."

Without thinking, I uttered, "You're right. It isn't."

He groaned. "Shit, now I don't wanna leave, but if I don't, we won't get this car out, and the dick fucked it up even more." His chair was shifted back, meaning he stood. A finger trailed down my cheek. "Will you be here next Saturday?"

"I think so."

"I'll see you then, sugar."

The following Saturday, my sister dropped me off. When I walked to the counter, the guy behind it said, "I have a message for you. Blue's sorry he can't make it, but he hopes you'll try to come back Monday and he'll be here."

I smiled wide and nodded my thanks. Since I was at the

café, I still had to sit and wait for my sister, so I ordered an iced coffee and blueberry muffin.

Even though I knew he wasn't coming, my heart still thumped hard every time the front door opened. Once my sister turned up, I was relieved; my poor heart needed the break. She led me out to the car and told me to get in.

"How was your day?" I asked Amy.

"Fine. Look, I'm not in the mood to chit-chat, just…zip it, okay?"

Sighing quietly so she wouldn't get upset by it, I nodded. I sat back in my seat, thought of a certain man and contemplated how I was going to make it there on Monday.

I waited until the next day before I spoke to my sister. Amy was sitting in the living room. I made my way from my room down the hall, with my hands on the walls to guide me. In the living room, I counted the five steps to the couch; only I didn't get there. Instead, I tripped and fell to the carpeted floor on my hands and knees.

"What are you doing?" Amy yelled.

"Sorry, I um… tripped." I felt around on the floor to see what had been laying there to trip me, but my hands ran over nothing but the carpet.

"There's nothing there. Get up," Amy snapped. I did, and I reached out to the couch and climbed from my knees to sit on it. "Was there something you wanted? Usually, you stay in your room."

Nodding, I asked, "I was hoping you could take me to the café on Monday."

"Why?" she huffed.

"I… um, I have to meet someone there."

"I'll see, okay? I have a lot to do to keep us fed and a roof over our heads."

She'd said that to me many times. I'd questioned her about it on a few occasions because I was sure our parents would have helped provide for us after their deaths. Not that I would want it, but since I was disabled, we needed it even more.

Our parents were well off, so every time Amy would hiss back, 'They never left enough for all *your* hospital bills,' I never could understand that.

I knew I was a burden to her, so I nodded and said, "Okay, Amy," even though everything inside me told me to fight with her, to demand she take me because God knew I didn't ask for much.

Still, I said no more, knowing one day, I would have to get out from under my sister and learn to live again.

Monday came and went. Amy said she was too busy to take me, and when I suggested a taxi, she yelled at me for wanting to waste our money on something so unnecessary. I felt terrible that I couldn't inform Blue I wouldn't be there like he had me. We didn't have a home phone; the only phone we had was Amy's mobile, and she had taken that with her.

If I had a friend, I would have called one, but they all soon disappeared after the accident.

I could only hope he would be there on Saturday and would understand my situation.

Wednesday night, Amy came home from work and told me to get on a warmer coat because she needed to go food shopping. She only liked me to come so I could push the trolley. She hated doing it and laughed if I crashed into anything.

At the supermarket, I trolled along slowly while Amy took off ahead. Thankfully, the place was lit bright enough for me to see her shadowed, blurred form in front of me.

"Rinda, stay there. I'm just going to grab some stuff. You're going too slowly. I'll be quicker on my own."

There was no point saying anything; her footsteps were already departing the aisle.

I felt awkward just standing there, so I turned to the shelves and pretended to look at what was in front of me. I didn't know how long I had been standing there, but suddenly, there was heat at my back and a whisper in my ear, "Why are you searching the condoms, sugar?"

No, God no. Blue was right behind me, and apparently, I was looking at condoms.

"Um," was all I could say.

"Were you thinkin' of buying them for me?"

Oh, my God!

Again, my reply was, "Um,"

He chuckled deeply. "I'm only teasin', baby," he uttered against my neck, and I swear he drew in a deep breath.

With his hands on my hips, he turned me. I looked up his blurred form toward his head and smiled shyly, knowing there was heat in my cheeks.

"Where were you Monday, Clary?" he asked, his hands still on my hips, making it hard for me to concentrate.

"Um, I-I'm sorry, Blue. I couldn't make it, and I had no way of telling you."

"Sugar, I'm gonna tell you straight up. I wanna see more of you. You willin' for that to happen?"

"Yes," I responded immediately. Hell, did that sound too keen?

"Best fuckin' word. What's your number? I gotta jet, but I need your number, baby."

I rattled off my sister's mobile and then added, "It was nice seeing you."

"You, too. Fuck, you, too. Take care, sugar, and we'll talk soon, yeah?"

"Yes." I smiled.

Later that night, I ended up telling my sister all about Blue.

I think she could tell how excited I was when I talked about him, but I got nothing from her other than, "We'll see if he rings. Not many men would want such a burden in their life, Rinda. I hope you know that."

Deflated, I went back to my room, hoping Blue would prove my sister wrong.

CHAPTER TWO

ONE MONTH LATER

CLARINDA

I was sitting in the passenger seat of the car, waiting for my sister while she ran an errand. It was a month after I saw Blue at the supermarket. He hadn't called, so I guessed my sister had been right. He hadn't even shown the times I went to the café again. Why did he act as though he liked me enough to call? Had I said something that night in the supermarket to change it? No, I couldn't have; he was the one who asked me for my number. I shook my head, attempting to shake the thoughts away.

The sun was shining brightly in the car that late afternoon, so I wound down my window to let the breeze through. The sounds of the outside world grew louder with vehicles driving near our parking spot at the side of the road. People walked up and down the pathway beside the car. I only wished I could see it. Unfortunately, like always, my eyes only managed a shadowy outline of things.

I tilted my head toward the breeze more and saw an outline of a building. What that building was, I had no clue.

Soon, I found myself blinking away tears as I thought of my most recent doctor's appointment, which I had just the day before. Even though I had been seeing that doctor for nearly four years, I still felt uncomfortable around him. His touch left me feeling dirty for some reason. Though, my sister swore he was the best in town and was the perfect doctor to try and help us fix my eyes.

Three years later, and I was still waiting for the right answer.

His words from yesterday ran through my mind. *"You're coming along fine, Clarinda. Just give it time."*

Time was all I had.

Amy still refused to let me work, to let me do anything, really. If I tried, we ended up in an argument. I was born an independent yet shy woman, and I was sick of relying on my sister for help. I was twenty-four, for god's sake.

I shifted in my seat, so my head was closer to the window and wondered why my sister was taking so long. She said she'd only be a moment.

"What the fuck are you looking at?" I heard yelled in a harsh voice from somewhere close.

Ignoring it, I went back to blinking at nothing until a dark form loomed in front of me. I jumped, hitting my head on the car roof.

"I said, what the fuck are you looking at, bitch?" A shadow of a manly-shaped hand reached in and gripped my hair, pulling my head toward the window.

"Please, please," I begged. "I wasn't staring at anything."

"You wanna be up in my business, watching what went down? I'll give you a better taste of it, slut." He shook my head roughly with the hand still in my hair.

I reached up with both hands and grabbed his wrist, trying to pull free. "I didn't see anything. I *can't* see anything. Please, I'm blind. You've got it wrong."

"Bullshit. I don't give a fuck either way." He jerked my head again, and it banged into the top of the window frame. His stinking, hot breath blew against my face as he leaned closer. "You are a looker. I think a lesson needs to be learned."

"No!" I yelled. "Please." My body shook with fright.

My hands sweated and my heart leaped from the thought of what could happen. *Amy, please hurry, please!*

"Shut the fuck up," he hissed. Suddenly, my hair was freed, and I flopped back ungracefully. My hands felt for the seat as I straightened myself.

What now? Dread filled my stomach. I didn't know what was going on, why all of a sudden he was silent, but then came the sound of my door being opened, causing me to jump. I threw my arms out in front of me, waving them around.

"No, please!" I cried.

A hand clamped around my thigh, his grip painful. "Come on, bitch. Take off your pants and spread 'em." He tugged on my sweatpants. My hands fought his hold.

"Stop, no. Stop. Amy!" I yelled.

He kept swatting my hands away and grumbling about something under his breath.

Then I heard another manly call, and then a thumping sound. The hands which were on me fell away.

"Leave her alone, Henry," the new person growled.

"Fuck off, Blue. This is none of your business."

Blue?

"I think it is. The lady doesn't want to be touched. If you don't back the hell off, I'll make you."

"Shit, she wasn't worth it anyway," the first man grumbled.

Silence, and then retreating footsteps. With shaking hands, I felt for the door to close it, but my hands came against a hard, warm wall. Bouncing back in my seat, I retracted them quickly.

"You all right, sugar?" my saviour asked.

Blue. Oh, God, it *was* Blue.

I nodded. Clenching my trembling hands, I whispered, "Yes." I was still tense, unsure if I was completely safe.

The thump of my door closing had me jumping once again. "He won't bother you again. You waitin' on someone?"

"My sister," I whispered.

Does he not remember me?

My heart plummeted. Maybe he didn't want to recognise me. That could be why he didn't call. I never left a good enough impression on him for him to care.

"Why didn't you call me?" I bravely asked through the silence.

"I did, Clarinda. I was told you didn't want anything to do with me."

My eyes widened. "No… I-I'd never say that, Blue."

"Fuck. Your sister…."

My heart pounded into my throat as the driver's side door opened beside me. I turned to it as my sister spat, "What have you done now, Clarinda?"

Tears pooled in my eyes. The adrenaline rush I had started to wear off. "Nothing, Amy. This…." I gestured with my hand in the general direction of the man I had thought of so frequently, "….is Blue. Um, I've talked about him. He, ah, just now helped me. Someone tried to attack me."

She snorted. "You probably brought it on yourself."

"She didn't," Blue clipped. My heart warmed.

"Whatever," Amy responded and started the car.

"You going to be okay?" he asked.

I nodded and looked toward the window. "I think so." I reached my hand out. He must have sensed I was having trouble finding him, so he placed his hand in mine. I squeezed it, my heart beat faster from the warmth and thrill of touching him. "Thank you," I whispered. "Can… would you meet me at the café? I'll be there next Saturday."

"I'll be there, sugar. Count on it." I could hear the smile in his voice. It had my cheeks heating and an urgent need to actually see him. I desperately wished to know what he looked like, what he felt like under my touch. I'd lay awake countless nights debating the colour of his eyes, not knowing if they were light or dark. While I'd heard his smile when he spoke, I was eager to see it and half-expected to find a dimple. Regardless of what he would look like to the outside world, none of it really mattered. His voice alone held me captive. As long as a man was kind to his woman like my father was to my mother, nothing else mattered.

"Hand in the car. We've got to go," Amy said.

I hadn't realised I was still gripping Blue's hand, but once I let go, I felt the warmth from his hold disappear. The reality of what happened slipped into my mind, and the smile fell from my face. Before I could say any more to Blue, Amy put the car into drive and took off.

I wanted her to turn the car around so I could find that warmth again, find the safety I felt around a man I hardly knew. I curled my arms around my waist, leaned my head back and closed my eyes thinking of the sweet yet hard, delicious tone of Blue's voice and found some comfort from it.

"What were you thinking, talking to a stranger?"

Sighing, I turned my head toward my sister. "He's not a stranger, Amy. He did help me." I shuddered at the thought of that dirty man touching me. "A man was attacking me."

"Well, what did you do for that to happen?"

"Nothing," I uttered.

"See, this is why you need me around all the time. You keep getting into trouble, and in the end, *I* keep having to save you."

Only that time, it wasn't her.

However, she was right. Over the past six months, I'd had many little accidents, and Amy had always been there for me. I had to admit—if Blue hadn't shown up, at least I knew my sister would have. She was always there.

Though, the accident which had just occurred was the worst I'd ever had... if I could call it an accident. The others before that were small incidents—a trip, a burn, stubbing my toe—and I'd been abused verbally many times on the street.

Still, it all gave me enough pause to think about how I would be lost without Amy. It actually made me sick to my stomach at the thought of fending for myself while in my condition. Yes, we annoyed each other, and yes, she could be downright mean, but she changed her ways to fit me into her life when I was nineteen and she was twenty-two. Without her, I wouldn't have had much of a life at all.

Okay, that wasn't entirely true.

People who were completely blind and saw nothing but blackness still coped. They used their other senses or had the help of guide dogs. There were many possibilities. I'd even suggested all those things to my sister at the start, told her I wanted to live on my own and learn to live with my disability. She wouldn't have it.

After what happened a few moments before, I wasn't sure I was ready to do any of that anymore.

I was scared something like that could happen again.

What would I do if I was on my own, walking down the street, and I didn't know someone was following me? I could turn a wrong corner and be trapped. I could witness something I never knew I was observing and be in a mess like I was earlier. So many things could happen. It was hard being with my sister all the time, but the thought of being without her scared me more.

At least I had my daily outings to the library while Amy worked. Those I really enjoyed, especially since I hardly sat on my own anymore. Not that it bothered me to sit on my own; at least I was able to listen to so many wonderful stories. Until, that was, Julian decided he had to know me. That had been about four months before. From that day forward, I would get several visits in the library from him.

He made me laugh, he made me smile, and the world seemed that much brighter with him around in it.

I also met his friend, Deanna, who works there. That had only been in the past two months, and still, we hadn't encouraged each other to talk openly. I was slowly warming up to her, but it was hard because of how snappy and annoyed she seemed to be all the time. The customers usually got a reprieve from her mouth, but if she came over to the table to grumble about something, look out. I had never in my twenty-four years heard a woman swear so much in my life. What was comical about it, though, was when Julian would bait her, she'd get frustrated and tell him where to go…explicitly. Julian didn't care. I loved to hear their interactions. Anyone could tell the 'family love' they had for each other.

At least I have someone *who's happy to see me.*

I turned my head toward Amy as she drove. Knowing my sister, her brows would be drawn, her jaw would be clenched, and her hands would be tight around the steering wheel. She was annoyed by me, for the attention I received but didn't want. I was her embarrassment.

Why had she told Blue I didn't want anything to do with him when he called? Was she jealous? Or maybe she just didn't want to see me hurt?

I wasn't sure, and I didn't want to ask. It would just end in a fight.

Everything was so confusing. One moment, I wanted to be independent and try to make Amy see I could do things for myself, and then the next, I found myself scared of what it would be like without her.

Confusion didn't accurately describe the chaos of my emotions.

I wanted to fight back and have my independence, and I wanted my sister to treat me with respect instead of a piece of poo under her shoe...then again, I was scared of so many things, which was why I clammed up so many times and said nothing, even though I regretted it every time.

However, what I *was* confident about was that Amy wasn't simply annoyed at me; rather, she truly hated me.

That hurt more than what the foul-breathed man tried to do to me.

My sister, my own family, hated me because I was useless. At least, that was how I felt.

ALSO BY LILA ROSE

Hawks MC: Ballarat Charter

Holding Out (FREE) Zara and Talon

Climbing Out: Griz and Deanna

Finding Out (novella) Killer and Ivy

Black Out: Blue and Clarinda

No Way Out: Stoke and Malinda

Coming Out (novella) Mattie and Julia

Hawks MC: Caroline Springs Charter

The Secret's Out: Pick, Billy and Josie

Hiding Out: Dodge and Willow

Down and Out: Dive and Mena

Living Without: Vicious and Nary

Walkout (novella) Dallas and Melissa

Hear Me Out: Beast and Knife

Breakout (novella) Handle and Della

Fallout: Fang and Poppy

Standalones related to the Hawks MC

Out of the Blue (Lan, Easton, and Parker's story)

Out Gamed (novella) (Nancy and Gamer's story)

Outplayed (novella) (Violet and Travis's story)

Romantic comedies

Making Changes

Making Sense

Fumbled Love

Trinity Love Series

Left to Chance

Love of Liberty (novella)

Paranormal

Death (with Justine Littleton)

In The Dark

CONNECT WITH THE AUTHOR

Webpage: www.lilarosebooks.com
Facebook: http://bit.ly/2du0taO
Instagram: www.instagram.com/lilarose78/
Goodreads:
www.goodreads.com/author/show/7236200.Lila_Rose

CPSIA information can be obtained
at www.ICGtesting.com
Printed in the USA
LVHW080818200222
711543LV00022B/2570

9 780648 481683